TILTON UNIVERSITY

BLAZE

CHASE LOVETT WANTS ME

Chase Lovett.
Star of my (unrequited) fantasies.
Hottest guy on campus.
Hockey god.

Too bad he has no idea who I am. Literally, I'm so invisible to him that he once sat on me in class.

No thanks to a fire in the dorms, he just became my accidental roommate.

Did I mention the hotel room our university moved us to has only one bed? *Not ideal.*

Worse, I accidentally left "My Precious" Lord of the Rings underwear hanging to dry in our shower.
My actual nightmare.

My name is Cammie Lovelock and this might just be the worst, best thing that's ever happened to me.

19

CHASE LOVETT WANTS ME

NEW YORK TIMES BESTSELLING AUTHOR
HELENA HUNTING

CHASE LOVETT WANTS ME CAST

CHASE LOVETT

TILTON BLAZE FORWARD

SIBLINGS
Channing & Chanel

PARENTS
Maxine & Cornel

TILTON BLAZE TEAMMATES

BRODY STILES

Tilton Blaze Forward
Chase's best friend and roommate

GAGE STEELE

Tilton Blaze Forward
Friend of Chase and Brody.
Live in the same dorm

MAC MEYERS

Tilton Blaze Enforcer
Friend of Chase, Brody and Gage
Second year, lives off campus

CAMMIE LOVELOCK

CHASE'S NEW OBSESSION

SIBLING
Essie

PARENTS
Athena & Demetrius

TILTON U FRIENDS

OPHELIA ROSE

Online Fanfic bestie, high school senior
Applied to Tilton for fall

TALLY VANDER ZEE

Tilton U Friend
In the same English class
Friends with Cammie's older sister

Published by Helena Hunting
Cover Design by Hang Le
Cover Image by @searland_art
Developmental Edit by Becca Mysoor Fairy Plotmother
Editing by Sarah Plocher of All Encompassing Books
Erica Russikoff of Erica Edits
Proofing by Julia Griffis
And Amanda of Drafthouse Editorial Services
Fore Edge Formatting by Kingdom Covers

ACKNOWLEDGMENTS

Husband and kidlet, I adore you. You inspire me every day and I'm so grateful for your love.

Deb, I adore you. Thank you for always having my back.

Becca, it is such an honor to know you, as a friend, as a badass fairy plotmother, as a strong, amazing businesswoman. Thank you for always challenging me and giving me the chance to learn new things.

Kimberly, thank you for all you do. It's been an amazing decade and I'm excited for what's next.

Sarah Pie, I honestly couldn't do this without you. You've been such a huge source of support and friendship and I'm so thankful to have you on my side.

My Alpha Beta team, you help make my stories better, thank you for being in this with me.

Catherine, Jessica F, Tricia and Tijan your kindness and wonderful energy are such a source of inspiration, thank you for your friendship.

Sarah, Erica, Amanda, Julia, thank you so much for working on this project with me, I know it was a beast, and I'm so honored to be able to work with you and helping me make it sparkle.

Sarah, Kate and Rae, thank you for being graphic gurus. Your incredible talent never ceases to amaze me.

Beavers, thank you for giving me a safe place to land, and for always being excited about what's next.

Influencers and review crew, you're amazing and I love your zeal for all things romance!

Kat, Marnie, Krystin; thank you for being such incredible women. I'm so thankful for your friendship.

Readers, bloggers, bookstagrammers and booktokers, thank you for sharing your love of romance and happily ever afters.

For the observers.
The introverts.
The quiet ones.
The bravest.

CHAPTER 1

CAMMIE

My phone pings with a message from my sister.

ESSIE

Video chat in 1 min!

I nearly collide with another person as I rush out of the communal bathroom. I flatten myself against the wall as Chase Lovett, hockey god, the most popular guy in our residence building and the hottest guy in first year, brushes past me without so much as a glance in my direction. Like I don't exist. It's basically the story of my life.

I continue my cardboard cutout impression as Chase, his hockey buddies, and two girls who haven't spoken a word to me in the two months we've lived on this floor, continue down the hall, laughing and chatting. They're probably heading to the common room. The Toronto Terror, the local pro hockey team, are playing tonight. I stare shamelessly at Chase's retreating form, all six-foot-four of dark hair, broad shoulders, and magnificent, highly smackable ass.

My phone rings, so I quickly hold my lanyard to the lock and slip into my room.

Aragorn, Legolas, and Arwen stare intensely at me from the poster above my bed.

"Hey! Hi! Hello!" I say breathlessly as Essie's two-dimensional image appears.

My room is directly across the hall from the bathroom, so I have no reason to be breathless. Chase does it to me every time.

"Did I catch you at a bad time?" A slight frown tugs at the corners of my sister's lips.

"Nope. Not a bad time. I was in the bathroom."

"Oh. Fair." She lobs a series of questions at me. "How are things? How are classes? Have you made any new friends since we talked last week?"

She asks the new friends question all the time. Essie and I are opposites. She's effortlessly cool, outgoing, and has an endless supply of friends. I'm nerdy, introverted, and have two close friends, one of whom I met online. The other I met in my English class. It took me six weeks to say hi. Her name is Tally, and she's the only person I know, who isn't a grandpa, who loves Good & Plenty.

Essie's phone is propped in a holder on her vanity, which is covered in makeup and application tools. Her straight, dark hair is pulled up in a messy bun on top of her head. She's wearing a pink, off-the-shoulder sweater and dark-wash denim.

"Classes are good." Especially the two I have with Chase. "And I talked to a girl in bio class last week." I asked if the seat was taken beside her. She said she was waiting for her friend. I found another one.

"That's great! What's her name?"

I scramble for a name. "Her name is Greta."

"That's old school. Have you made plans yet? Did you exchange numbers?" Essie dips a liner brush in black liquid, expertly lining her dark eyes with a dramatic flourish.

"Not yet. But I'll see her tomorrow." It's not untrue. I will see her tomorrow. But I will not be asking to exchange numbers or hang out. I sat three rows back and watched her friend slide into the seat next to her. I've seen her with Chase before. Just talking, but still. We definitely don't run in the same circles. If I had a chance in hell with Chase, she would be competition.

"That's cool. Have you seen Brody on campus yet?" Essie asks. "I know a couple of other people on campus if you want their info."

"Oh, that's okay. You don't need to do that." Like I want my sister making my friends for me. "And, yeah. We have a class together." I fight to keep my internal cringe from showing on my face. I've managed to keep that tidbit to myself up until this moment. Brody Stiles is the youngest brother of Tristan Stiles, pro hockey player for the Toronto Terror.

Essie has always sort of known the Stiles brothers because of her best friend Rix, and I've always known *of* them. Tristan, Nate, and Brody. Brody and I are the same age, just like Essie is the same age as Brody's middle brother, Nate. But until this year, my path had never really crossed with Brody.

Essie stops applying makeup to shoot me a disbelieving look. "What? Why didn't you tell me that until now?"

"It's Intro to Bio. There are like a thousand people in that class." It's held in one of the biggest lecture theaters on campus. However, I only noticed Brody because he was with Chase, who's impossible *not* to notice. Chase is bigger than life, has more charisma in his left pinkie than I do in my entire body, and is drop-dead gorgeous. They also both live on the same floor as me in residence. How I managed to end up living with hockey royalty is beyond me. My sister is unaware of this fact, and I plan to keep it that way. I don't need her to try to matchmake my friendships, swooping in to save me like some ethereal cool to my awkward weird.

But I'm not complaining about the number of times I've seen a shirtless guy wrapped in a white towel walking from the bathroom back to their dorm room so far this year.

"Have you introduced yourself to Brody?" Essie presses.

"I've said hi." A total of three times, while passing him in the hall. Brody always initiates. Sometimes I get the sense he's more like me. Not nerdy, per se, but quiet. Introverted. Like all the attention the sport he excels at is a burden and not a flex.

"Good. Brody's a sweetheart." Essie continues fixing her makeup. "How's that submission for creative writing coming along?"

"Oh, it's coming," I lie again.

"I can have a look at it for you before you hand it in," she offers.

"I still have a bit more work to do. And they have services here for that." By a bit more work, I mean that I have ninety percent left. All I've completed so far is the opening paragraph. Every time I sit down to write it, my brain takes a trip down No Thank You Lane into Let's Write Fanfic Instead Ville.

Essie stops to give me a disapproving look. "Please tell me you've started."

"I've started." One paragraph. "You know how I am. I'm good under pressure. I'll get it done." It's not due until the end of the semester; I have loads of time to procrastinate.

"I'm here to help. Just let me know if you need a set of eyes or a brainstorming session."

"Thanks, Ess. Where are you headed tonight?" I prop my chin on my fist as my sister changes into a slinky, gold tank top with spaghetti straps. She's braless with Band-Aids over her nipples. I wish I had a speck of her confidence.

"Sahar Jordan, who played Lila on *The Way We Weren't*, is throwing a party. I couldn't say no to the invite, because of course I want to see what her house looks like. Also, all the sexiest people in the city will be there, and I need to make more contacts again."

"Sounds like a blast." And the very last place I would ever want to be. "Are you happy to be back in Toronto?" Essie has been working as a makeup artist in Vancouver for the past two years. But she recently accepted a contract in Toronto. Rix is getting married next summer, and Essie is the maid of honor and wants to be here for all the planning.

"Not excited about the winter, but happy to be close to you and Rix and Mom and Dad again."

"I'm happy about that, too."

"One of these weekends, you have to come out and meet all the Terror girls. They're so much fun. We could go to the campus café, and I could introduce you to—"

"Sounds like a plan." And a lot of social anxiety. But I'd do it to spend time with my sister. And if Rix is there, it'll be less awkward.

"Okay, little sister. I have to run, but we'll talk again later this week?"

"Sure."

"Hey, are you going out tonight?" Essie asks this every time. The answer is always a lie.

"I'm hanging out with friends in the common room later."

"Good. Great. I told you university would be good for you! Love you, Cam." She makes a kissy face.

"Love you, too, Ess."

She ends the call and I flop back in my computer chair.

My stomach grumbles obnoxiously. I haven't eaten since lunch. It's six fifty-seven. Which means I've missed dinner in the good cafeteria and all I can order is a crappy burger or a sub. Neither is appealing. But the common room has a kettle so I can make ramen.

Do I have a kettle in my room? Of course. And a microwave and a mini fridge.

But if I go to the common room, I'll likely see Chase. And Brody, which would make my sister happy. They're practically glued to each other's sides. Unless there's a girl hanging off Chase, which is ninety percent of the time. But I could still see Chase. Watch the game (him) for a few minutes while I make ramen. If I'm lucky, there will be a line and I'll have to hang out for twenty minutes or so. It's happened before.

Decision made, I spend the next twenty minutes changing into every outfit I own and decide my jeans and black hoodie with a Middle-Earth icon on the back is the best I can do. I attempt cat eyes via my sister's video tutorial, but I fail three times and give up. I go with two swipes of mascara and some gloss, shove my feet into my shoes, forget my ramen and have to go back to my room, then head to the common room.

As predicted, there's a line at the kettle, three deep. This is perfect. Especially since Chase and all his hockey buddies are exactly where I expected them to be: sitting on the couch in front of the TV watching the Terror game.

The girls who always look through me are perched on the arms of the couch, one next to Chase, the other next to Gage, one of Chase and Brody's other teammates. Brody is sitting on the floor in a gaming chair.

I join the line for the kettle.

And while I wait, I observe.

Chase is wearing faded denim and a Terror T-shirt. His dark hair is damp, like he's fresh from the shower. I bet he smells incredible. His thickly muscled bicep flexes as he high-fives Brody when 44, Brody's brother, scores a goal.

Brody wears jeans, black boots, and a black hoodie with the phrase "I'd rather be on the ice" in tiny letters across his heart. Gage is dressed in red workout gear. There is a decent chance he came here directly from the gym and smells like sweat and sneakers. It's fairly common, and his friends often razz him about it.

The guy in front of me moves closer to the kettle and I close the gap. Two more people making cheap food for dinner and then it's my turn.

Chase stands and spins to face the back, an unmade cup of KD in his hand.

The guy beside me yells, "Send it my way. I got you covered, Lovett!"

Chase tosses the KD cup in my direction.

For a fraction of a second, my eyes lock with Chase's. My heart skips two beats. My entire body tingles from head to toe. My breath catches in my lungs.

I'm holding my ramen cup, my soya sauce, and a pair of chopsticks. And the KD cup is coming straight for me. A hand shoots out from my right and catches the KD before it hits me in the face, covering up Chase's flared eyes.

And then one of the girls who always looks through me comes shrieking into the room, yelling about a party tonight at some fraternity house after the game.

I tell myself I'm glad I've never been invited to a party.

It sounds like way too many people and too many bad decisions.

I make my ramen and steal one last glance at Chase before I head back to my room, leaving the guy behind me to make Chase's dinner.

I should definitely work on the creative writing submission. It would be the smart thing to do. The right thing.

But I have this great party scene in my head for my fanfic. I flip open my laptop. It shouldn't take me long to get it down. Then I'll focus on my submission.

CHAPTER 2

CHASE

"If you could get picked up by any team, what team would it be?" Gage asks.

"That's easy, Toronto," I reply. "Brodes, what team would you want to play for?" Brody has already been drafted and so have I. But Ottawa has their eye on him, and Vancouver wants me.

"Anywhere but Toronto." Brody tosses a stress ball into the air with one hand and catches it with the other.

"But playing for the same team as your brother would be so cool," Gage says. "You've got those good Stiles genetics."

"Yeah, but the pressure would be stupid. And he would want to mentor me, or challenge me, and then it would just be me trying to mirror his career and that would suck. I'll already always be compared to him." Brody bounces the ball on his elbow, catches it, then repeats the move on the other side.

Tristan is one of the top players in the league, so I can see how much of a double-edged sword this is for Brody. I have an older sister and a younger brother, neither of which are into sports, so there's no one to compete with.

We leave the locker room and are immediately rushed by a group of girls hanging out in the arena foyer. I don't know them, but two of them seem to know Gage. Brody tucks his hands in his pockets and plasters on a smile, but this shit always makes him uncomfortable. His brother had a reputation last year, until Tristan started dating his teammate's sister. Now he's in a committed relationship. But the rumors still follow him around. And because Brody plays hockey and looks like a younger version, people expect him to be the same way.

One of the girls turns to me and starts chatting as we head for the exit. I'm pretty sure I've seen her at a party before. Brody and I have the same class next, so we make our way to the science building while Gage heads to Rocks for Jocks with the two girls. A rush of students floods the stairs to the lecture theater. We fist-bump guys and accept hugs from girls. It's like this wherever we go. Hockey is what Tilton University is known for, so we're basically royalty. It doesn't matter that we're freshmen, plus Brody's brother instantly elevates our status.

I've never been this high on the social food chain and while I've enjoyed the hell out of it for the past couple of months, it's becoming repetitive. Every weekend it's another party, another hookup, another girl's number in my phone who I don't connect with in any way other than physically. They don't want to know me anyway. They want to talk about pro hockey players and my dream car when I secure my first contract.

I glance to the right, where a pint-sized girl with a hood covering half her face climbs the stairs next to me. Someone on their phone nearly collides with her, but she pulls a Matrix move and ducks out of the way. She mutters "excuse you too, dick-face" and continues up the steps. We reach the doors at the same time. I raise my arm above her head—it's not hard, she's at least a foot shorter than me—and leave enough room for her to pass through the gap.

She pauses, head turning, chin tipping up. Gray eyes lift to meet mine. I feel her gaze like a shot of tequila to my soul. And other parts.

"After you." I motion her ahead of me.

Her eyes flare. Her mouth opens and closes. Someone almost bumps into her from behind. Other bodies stream past us. She murmurs a barely audible *thank you* and scurries past me. I lose her in the crowd, disappointed because she has a face I want to keep looking at.

Class is long. And today we're talking about cell structure, so I'm forced to take copious notes, in part because I only managed to read half the chapter in preparation. After class, Brody and I meet up with a few of our teammates to talk strategy for the upcoming game before we return to the dorms.

I should stay in tonight and study. Catch up on my reading for bio and get to bed early. But the second we walk through the doors, Annabelle and Barbie are there, telling us about another off-campus party.

"Cover is only like twenty bucks, and they have a keg and coolers," Barbie says.

"And if you're on the hockey team, they said they'll let you in for free," Annabelle adds.

These two are always around. Always. Wherever we go, they go. We don't invite them; they just show up and tag along. I don't dislike them. But I don't particularly like them either. None of us have ever expressed an interest in hooking up with them. I always get the sense if someone made that mistake, these two would immediately declare girlfriend status and it would be four more years of them always being around. Currently, they function as a semi-deterrent for other girls, which Brody isn't completely against because he's hung up on some high school crush he's never gotten over, so I tolerate them.

"I'm game, how about you guys?" Gage says.

Gage is always up for a party. It's a big part of the reason he's already skating the academic probation line.

I shrug and look to Brody. He shrugs back.

I glance to the right, where a pint-sized girl wearing a hoodie with the phrase "social battery on empty" scrawled under a frowning battery over her chest speed walks toward the elevators. Could it be the same girl from class earlier today? She jams her thumb on the button.

"Come on! It's a nice night. Soon it'll be snow and crappy weather and we'll have to go to bars instead. It'll be fun!" Annabelle whines.

"I'm not staying late," Brody says.

"Me neither."

"Yay!" Barbie and Annabelle jump around while clapping. "Let's get changed and meet down here in twenty minutes!"

We move as a group toward the elevators.

Gage rushes for them, trying to get there before the doors slide closed. The elevators take forever here. The girl at the front lifts her head as she reaches for the panel inside.

Thick dark lashes, gray eyes rimmed in charcoal. I swear it's the girl from my class this morning. But the doors close before I can confirm her identity.

CHAPTER 3

CAMMIE

"That's right, Cammie, don't be shy. Tell me exactly what you want," Chase whispers against my lips, his hand gliding down my stomach.

"Don't stop touching me." I run my fingers through his dark, silky hair. "Or kissing me."

His luscious, full lips curve into a panty-melting smile as he circles my navel. He opens his mouth, and a horrible, shrill sound comes out of it.

The dream dissolves and my eyes pop open as the fire alarm blares through the building. "For fuck's sake, it was just getting to the good part." I pull my pillow over my head and groan. Why, even in my dreams, can't I be forward and explicit with my direction? I should have asked him to eat me out and pound me into the mattress. But no, all dream me can ask him to do is kiss and touch me.

It's the third time this week that the fire alarm has gone off in the middle of the freaking night. Maybe I can just lie here and pretend I don't exist until it's over.

"Everyone up and out! This is a real fire alarm!" A fist slams against my door. "I know you're in there. Get your ass out of bed!"

So much for pretending I don't exist.

Colby Barton, our floor RA, moves on to the next door. "You can't bring a suitcase with you, Fred. Grab a hoodie and let's go."

I throw off my covers and roll out of bed. It's one-oh-seven in the morning. Living on campus will be fun, Essie said. You'll love it, Essie said. She failed to mention this less than pleasant frequent occurrence. I rush to pull a hoodie over my T-shirt, tug on a pair of jeans, grab my backpack, toss the book on my nightstand inside, along with my phone, and shove my feet into my shoes. I throw my door open and am about to step into the hall when a giant, half-naked man body comes careening into my room. I stumble back to avoid being knocked off my feet, but trip over my own feet and wind up on my ass.

My mouth goes dry, and my palms and panties dampen as I take in the hulking form standing in the middle of my room. Chase is six-foot-four inches of hot-as-fuck hockey player. And he's *inside* my room. Every single part of me is immediately alert even though he doesn't even notice me sprawled out on the floor.

"Stiles and Lovett, stop messing around and get your asses outside! This is not a drill!"

"Sir, yes, sir." They salute Colby and hustle down the hall.

I pick myself up off the floor and shove my wallet into my backpack before I sling it over my shoulder and head for the door. But I pause to grab my laptop, just in case.

I join my floormates in the hall. The crowd has thinned considerably in the last minute. I'm halfway to the emergency exit stairs when the sprinklers come on.

The girls ahead of me shriek. The sprinklers are a first. I quickly shove my laptop under my hoodie to protect it. I really wish I'd put it in my backpack before leaving my room, but it's too late for that now.

I pull my hood up. Maybe this time it isn't just pizza burning.

I huddle close to the wall and get swept up in the sea of bodies. I rush down the stairs and out into the cool fall night.

Groups of students congregate outside the residence building, some still dressed, having just returned from a night out. Others, like me, are wearing wrinkled clothes pulled over pajamas. A few unfortunate girls are in sleep shorts and tanks, and a handful of guys are shirtless. A few weeks ago, it was warm enough for shorts, but fall has crept in, and the nights around here are cool.

It takes me less than two seconds to find Chase in the gaggle of groggy students. The star hockey player (and hero of my hormone-fueled dreams) is standing beside Brody and another guy whose name I don't know but whose face is familiar. I head for the closest empty bench, which also happens to be near Chase and his hockey buddies. I need to check my laptop for water damage, obviously.

One of the girls who clearly went out tonight based on her outfit, bounces over. "Chase! I thought you were coming to the keg party!"

I pause as I pull my laptop out from under my hoodie, jealous of how easy it is for her to talk to him. How casually she puts her hand on his bare arm. How brazenly her eyes rake over his bare chest on an appreciative sweep.

"That was tonight? We ended up playing a game of pickup." He tips his chin toward the building. "You know what the deal is?"

She shrugs. "Dunno. But we might go back to the party if it's gonna be a while. You can still come."

Chase frowns, attention shifting to Gage as he joins the group. "Why are you soaked?"

"The fucking sprinklers went off."

"What? When?" Chase asks.

Lightning zigzags across the sky as I inspect the state of my laptop. I need to be quick before it starts raining.

This newfound knowledge triggers panic from the keg party girl, and that panic spreads like a bad rumor as the fire truck pulls up. I'm more worried about being able to check my fanfic updates than I am the state of my clothes. Wet things dry. Unless they're electronic. I heave a sigh of relief when my laptop screen comes to life. I quickly close it, slide it into its protective sleeve, and put it in my backpack. I check a few of my fanfics on my phone, none of which have updated in the past two hours. I huddle into my damp hoodie and wish I'd thought to bring my pillow. Then at least I could curl up on this bench.

We've been out here for a freaking hour in the drizzling rain when I notice Colby, the RA, talking to one of the firefighters and a few other older adults. They're all frowning. Eventually one of them takes the megaphone, but their grim expression is not reassuring. "Attention, everyone! I need your attention!" He shouts three times before everyone finally shuts up.

I just want to go back to bed. I don't even care if it's wet.

"As I'm sure you know, there was a fire in the common area on the third floor that triggered the sprinkler system. Unfortunately, there was a technical issue with the sprinklers." He clears his throat. "And uh…it looks like it will be a couple of days before we're able to get everyone from the first three floors back into your rooms."

Angry chatter bursts from the crowd.

The guy with the megaphone has to ask for silence five times.

"I understand this is inconvenient, however, we've made arrangements with the hotel down the street to accommodate all of you."

That incites more questions about getting things out of rooms. A girl breaks down in tears. Some guy makes a joke about needing his condoms. I sigh and really wish I'd brought my pillow, because hotel ones are way too poofy and they give me a neck crick.

Megaphone man moves to the front of the pack and we

shamble as a herd down the street to the hotel, which is located at the edge of campus. We're halfway there when another bolt of lightning streaks across the sky. A sonic boom of thunder follows, and then the sky opens up. Within seconds, I'm completely drenched. And really freaking glad I put my laptop in its protective, water-resistant case.

CHAPTER 4

CHASE

"Dry clothes have been provided for you and are already in the room. They tried to make sure the sizes were accurate." Colby tips his head back and pushes his glasses up his nose. "Steele, you're in room 606 with Stiles."

Brody and Gage high-five.

Colby points at them and gives them his disapproving dad face. It would be a lot more convincing if he were less like a character from the set of *The Big Bang Theory*. He's a good guy, though, and he's just trying to maintain some order when there isn't any. "If I get so much as one noise complaint from your room, I'll tell your coach."

"We'll be on our best behavior. Scout's honor." Brody holds up two fingers.

Colby rolls his eyes and scans his clipboard. "Lovett, you're with…Lovelock in room 420."

"Who?"

"Cameron Lovelock."

I look to the guys. They just shrug.

"Never heard of him," I say.

Colby passes me the key. "Same goes for you about the noise complaints."

I salute him. "Sir, yes, sir."

He gives me an unimpressed look.

"We have practice in the morning," I remind him. We have practice almost every morning.

"I've heard that before."

We head for the elevators and wait with the other students who have been assigned rooms. We all look like a bunch of drowned rats. And I probably look like a colossal douche since I'm shirtless. But I'd literally just gotten out of the shower when the alarm went off. I hope Colby wasn't lying about the pajamas or I'll be turning a sheet into a toga until I get some clothes.

We cram ourselves into the elevator. Every button gets pushed. We should have taken the stairs. Two girls are huddled in the corner giggling behind their hands as they eye us from the side.

"You ask," one whispers.

"No, you."

"Yes. His brother plays for the Terror," I say helpfully.

"That's, like, so, so cool. And you all play for the school team, right?" one girl asks.

The elevator doors open, and they shuffle out onto the second floor.

Brody pulls his hood up and leans against the wall, avoiding eye contact with everyone.

We lose a few more people on the third floor.

"You wanna come up to our room for a bit and hang out?" Gage asks.

"Nah, man. It's late. Text in the morning and we'll grab breakfast, though?"

"Sure. Good luck with your roommate."

I get off on the fourth floor and tread down the hall to room 420. Hopefully this Cameron dude is chill. And not a complete fucking weirdo.

I scan my keycard and open the door. Sitting in the middle of the single king-sized bed is a small dude. He's wearing a school hoodie that's probably four sizes too big. The hood is pulled up, concealing his face, and his laptop is open in front of him. He types frantically. It's actually impressive how quickly his fingers move across the keyboard.

I let the door fall closed, expecting it to startle him, but he just keeps typing. It isn't until I'm standing at the end of the bed that he finally realizes he's not alone anymore.

His shriek is…high-pitched and feminine. He slams his laptop shut and yanks his hood down. Earbuds fall onto the laptop, which has a sticker that reads MY FAVORITE SPORT IS READING. I already feel judged. And that feeling magnifies as wide, gray eyes meet mine.

Wide, gray eyes, framed with thick dark *feminine* lashes.

Her long dark hair is pulled back in a braid that hangs over her shoulder. And her legs are bare. She's wearing a pair of socks pulled up to her knees, though. "Uh, I think maybe there's been a mistake. I'm supposed to be rooming with some guy named Cameron."

She blinks at me. And says nothing.

"Are you Cameron's girlfriend?" I ask.

She shakes her head.

I wait for her to offer more information, but nothing.

"Are you Cameron?"

She narrows her eyes, like I'm stupid for even asking.

This is getting awkward.

Her tongue darts out and drags across her full bottom lip.

I wait for her to say something. Anything. But all I get is more silence.

While we have this weird standoff, I take in the angles of her face. She has high cheekbones and a delicate nose. Her lips are full and pouty, and her chin is dainty. Her frame swims in the giant hoodie. I'm positive she's the same girl I spotted in class and getting on the elevator in my building last week.

I'm not sure how long I stand there, but eventually I thumb over my shoulder. "I'm just gonna…"

I back up toward the door and rush out of the room. Obviously, there's been some kind of mistake. I wait forever for the elevator to take me back to the lobby. Should have taken the stairs.

Some girl is freaking out. Like legit snot-sobbing all over the place. "You don't understand! If I don't have my creams, my face will be a mess by morning! I can't *not* have them. And it's not over the counter. It's a prescription and my whole life will be ruined without it!"

I approach Colby, but he holds up a hand. "Whatever your issue is, it'll have to wait until morning. I'm already dealing with enough."

A group of girls in the corner eye me. I'm not in the mood to be accosted, especially since I still don't have a fucking shirt. I avoid the elevator and run up six flights of stairs to Brody and Gage's room. I'm unsurprised to find them sprawled out on their beds watching hockey, surrounded by vending machine snacks.

"I have a problem."

"Is Cameron a serial killer?" Gage asks.

"No. Cameron's a girl."

"Have you hooked up with her before?" Brody's eyes are suddenly alight with excitement.

Of course he would be all kinds of gleeful about me ending up rooming with a past hookup. I'm not a total playboy, but I like sex, and girls like me, so I've enjoyed the perks of being on the hockey team and no parental guidance over the past couple of months. But lately, it's become…boring.

"No, dude. They obviously made a mistake, but Colby is dealing with drama so I couldn't explain the situation."

"Is she hot?" Brody asks.

"I mean, not in, like, a typical way."

"Does that mean she is or isn't hot?" Gage presses.

Gage has a very specific type. Either, off-limits like his math tutor. Or, since he can't have her, anyone who seems interested in him and a party, preferably at the same time.

"She's not your type." She has the kind of face you want to keep looking at because it's not like anyone else's. "Can I crash here?" They have two beds and no couch, but a single shitty computer chair and an old desk.

Gage looks at me like I've lost my mind. "Bro, we're all over six-two and these are double beds. No, you can't crash here, unless you want to sleep on the floor."

"Seriously? Hotel floors are gross."

"I'll sleep with Cameron." Brody brushes crumbs off his shirt as he sits up.

"No. That's not…" I shake my head. "No."

"So she is hot."

"Yeah, but she's weird. I showed up and tried to talk to her, and she just screamed then stared at me like I had two heads."

"Maybe she's an exchange student and English isn't her first language," Brody suggests.

"Her laptop had an English sticker on it."

"Maybe she's HOH and communicates through ASL," Gage offers. He's fluent in ASL because of his younger sister.

"Maybe? But she was wearing earbuds, so I don't think so. Could be wrong though."

Brody smirks. "Maybe your bare chest rendered her speechless."

"Fuck you guys. I'll see you in the morning."

"Have fun with Cameron!" Brody calls after me.

I take the elevator back to the fourth floor and stand outside the door to room 420. I shake out my hands and roll my head on my shoulders. "You got this. She's just a girl who thinks reading is a sport, for fuck's sake."

I tap my key against the sensor and open the door.

CHAPTER 5

CAMMIE

Chase appears in the room again. Still shirtless.

My entire body goes haywire as his eyes meet mine. *Chase Lovett is making intentional eye contact with me*. I pinch the inside of my arm just to make sure I'm awake. "I guess it wasn't a fever dream after all."

"You can talk." Chase stands half a dozen feet away with his hands propped on his narrow hips, every last one of his rippling, cut abs on display.

That sexy V of muscle teases my eyeballs, dragging them lower, to where his jogging pants ride seriously low.

But even in my dreams, I never get to the point where I touch what's underneath. Or see it. I also never get to the point where his hand goes down *my* pants. Dream Chase's fingers never glide over a bare nipple, and his dream mouth never makes it past my collarbones.

"Uh, yeah," I croak.

I'm actually speaking to Chase Lovett. Most popular guy in our dorm—maybe even the entire university. At least in first year. All the girls want to get with him. Including this wall-flower. And here he is, standing in front of me without a damn shirt, and all I can do is mutter a couple of words.

"Are you Cameron?"

"Yeah."

He nods and runs his hand through his thick, luscious locks. In my dreams, I've done that, too. "I tried to get Colby to switch me rooms, but it's all drama downstairs so we're stuck with each other for tonight at least. If I had somewhere else sanitary to go, I'd stay there."

If I could melt into the bed, I definitely would. "Sorry I'm not cool enough for you," I mumble. I should have accepted defeat an hour ago and called Essie, but it's officially the middle of the night.

His eyes flare. "Whoa. Hey. That's not what I meant." He holds up both hands. "I just mean that I'm a dude and they probably made the same mistake I did, thinking your name meant we both had swords instead of tulips."

"I'm sorry, what?"

"You know." He motions to his crotch. "Sword." Then he points to me with one hand and his mouth with the other. "Tulips."

I pull my hood over my head and roll onto my side, laughing uncontrollably.

"I'm not wrong," Chase grumbles.

It takes me a good two minutes to calm down enough to sit up. I wipe my eyes and sigh. "No, Chase, you are not wrong."

His brow quirks. "You know my name."

I roll my eyes. "Seriously? Every first year on campus knows who you are, and probably a good percentage of the second years, too." I close my laptop. I'm obviously not getting any more writing done tonight. "You know, if you don't like your roommate situation, all you have to do is go down to the lobby dressed as you are and I'm sure someone will invite you back to their room for party time."

"I have practice in the morning and that kind of party isn't good for my on-ice performance." He's so matter-of-fact about it.

"Right. Okay. Well, we should probably get the couch ready

so you can get your beauty sleep." Also, I've managed to string together a few coherent sentences and I'm probably reaching my limit.

I cross my fingers he has a chivalrous bone in his body and doesn't make me sleep on the pullout once it's set up. Chase pushes the coffee table out of the way while I remove the cushions. He steps in to pull it out. The springs creak ominously.

"That's not a reassuring sound."

"It probably hasn't been used in a while," I offer.

It's already made up with sheets, so all we have to do is grab the spare pillow and comforter from the closet. My palms are sweaty, and my imagination is in overdrive as we spread the duvet over the thin, shitty mattress. Never in a million years did I imagine I'd be making a bed with Chase Lovett. Or sleeping in the same room as him.

Our eyes meet across the bed. My vagina tingles and my mouth goes dry.

He runs a hand through his hair. "I'll take the couch."

"Oh." I wring my hands and give him my best innocent eyes. The couch looks terrifying. "Are you sure?"

He nods and glances longingly at the king bed before refocusing on the saggy pullout. "Yeah. For sure. It's just for one night."

"It can't be that bad, right?"

We both nod.

It's getting awkward again. "Do you want to use the bathroom first or should I?"

"You can go first, for sure."

I nervously rummage around in my backpack for my toothbrush and toothpaste. It's a leftover habit from my braces days. I disappear into the bathroom, heaving a huge sigh of relief as I close the door and flip the lock. I'm not sure how I'll survive a night in the same room with Chase. I basically dream about him at least twice a week. I sincerely hope I don't accidentally moan his name in my sleep.

I'm halfway through brushing my teeth when a huge crash startles me. I rush to unlock the door and poke my head into the room.

"For fuck's sake," Chase mutters.

Chase's feet and arms are raised in the air, his long body folded in half and stuck inside the gaping hole in the center of the pullout couch. He's busted right through the springs.

"Hold on! I'm coming to help!" I quickly spit my mouthful of toothpaste into the sink, use the sleeve of my new, excessively large school hoodie to wipe my mouth, and rush over to help. The mattress has sunk into the hole where the springs gave way. Stuffing and more springs poke out of the bottom. It sort of reminds me of a cartoon character stuck inside a Venus flytrap. He grabs the edges of the mattress to pull himself back out, but all it does is force him deeper into the hole.

"Stop flailing and give me your hand."

"I'm fine. I've got this."

"Really? Because it looks like you don't have this. At all. Just give me your hand." I extend one but have to push the extra-long sleeve up to my elbow for the seven hundredth time.

Chase tips his head back and gives me an appraising, doubtful look. "What do you weigh, a buck ten? How are you going to help?"

I roll my eyes. "Do you want to be stuck there all night or what?"

He takes my hand and I swear fireworks explode in my lady business. Chase tries to brace his other arm behind him, but all it does is break the bed more. It does create more space for him to move around in, though. Eventually one side of the mattress falls to the floor, allowing him to stand up and climb out of the destroyed sofa bed.

"Well, that's a giant piece of shit. They better not charge me for breaking it." Chase's fists are propped on his narrow hips again.

His hair is a delightful, rumpled mess, his face is red, and sweat beads on his temples. It's exactly how he looks in my dreams.

I avert my gaze back to the bed. "They'll probably think we had swing-from-the-rafters sex on it." The sudden additional awkwardness is as uncomfortable as an itchy wool blanket.

I can feel Chase's eyes on me. "Why the hell would we have swing-from-the-rafters sex on a shitty pullout couch when there's an enormous, probably super comfortable king bed right there?" He thumbs over his shoulder.

I keep my eyes fixed on the broken sofa bed. "So no one would have to sleep in the wet spot." Why can't I just keep my stupid mouth shut?

"That's actually a good point."

I glance at him out of the corner of my eye.

He pokes at his cheek with his tongue. "I can sleep in the tub or something."

I sigh. The king bed is huge. The tub would barely fit him. Plus, if I don't at least offer, I look like a jerk and he'll probably say mean things about me to his friends. "Or we could use pillows as a divider, and we can each have half of the bed." There, I've extended the offer. Essie would be proud.

"Deal." He yanks the comforter down and grabs the pillows from the floor, arranging them in a row down the middle. "We can even have our own comforters. What side do you usually sleep on? Left or right? I usually sleep on the right, but if that's your preferred side, you have it." He looks at me expectantly.

I shrug. Dorm beds are tiny so it's hard to say which side I gravitate to. "I can take the left."

"You're sure?"

"Yeah. I'm sure." He's still shirtless.

What if he gets into bed and he's wearing nothing but those pants? How will I sleep two feet away from him and his bare chest and his glorious muscles and exceptional hotness?

"There's an extra set of clothes in the bathroom," I blurt.

He runs his hand over his chest and glances at my bare legs.

"Cool. I'll just get ready." He spins around and heads for the bathroom. I watch the muscles in his back and admire his ass.

I definitely won't be getting much sleep.

While he's in the bathroom, I send a quick message to my best friend. We met online a year ago and both love *Lord of the Rings*. We've never met in person, but we exchange messages daily through our fanfic chat.

Earlier she asked if we were hit by the storm. I told her our dorm flooded thanks to the sprinklers, and now we were stuck in a hotel down the street for the foreseeable future.

@LEGAGORNSANDWICH

Remember the hockey player I'm lusting after?

@THEREALOPHELIA

How could I forget? Is he in the hotel with you?

@LEGAGORNSANDWICH

He's my roommate for the night.

@THEREALOPHELIA

Seriously????? HOW?

@LEGAGORNSANDWICH

Gender neutral first name. They made a mistake and put us together.

And there is only one bed.

@THEREALOPHELIA

OMG

OMFGGGGGGGGGG

Ride him like a bucking bronco.

@LEGAGORNSANDWICH

In my dreams. Literally.

The water stops running in the bathroom.

@LEGAGORNSANDWICH

He's coming out of the bathroom soon. Wish me luck.

@THEREALOPHELIA

Luck!

Channel your inner Arwen.

I shove my phone into my backpack and remember I'm not wearing pants. I quickly jam my legs into the pyjama pants they provided. Chase comes out of the bathroom while I'm trying to cinch them around the waist by pulling the drawstring as tight as it will go. I tie a quick bow, praying they'll stay where they are, but they slide down my legs and pool at my feet.

He rubs his full bottom lip. "Those are a little big on you, huh?"

I hold my fingers a fraction of an inch apart. "Just a touch."

He snickers.

I roll my eyes and chuckle. "Everything I came here in is still soaking wet."

"Yeah. I saw your stuff in the bathroom."

Horror hits me. My *Lord of the Rings* "My Precious" underwear is hanging on the shower rod.

I avoid looking at him and slide between the sheets, turning off the bedside lamp before I pull the covers up over my head. "Night."

"Night." The bed dips and he flicks off the other light, submerging us in darkness. He settles in, rustling around a bit, maybe trying to get comfortable while I lie here like a frozen corpse.

His breathing evens out in less than two minutes.

"Of course," I mutter.

He's one of those people whose head hits the pillow and two seconds later they're dead to the world. Essie is like that. So is my dad. I'm the person who has to read for an hour before my mind settles enough to allow sleep. But I can't read right now.

And I don't want to move and risk waking him. So I stare at the ceiling and pray to the Gods of Embarrassment that I don't dream about him tonight.

I must eventually pass out because when I wake, the clock is flashing, signaling the power went out. The wind howls outside, and rain continues to patter the window. It makes the already urgent need to pee that much more unbearable. I quietly slide out of bed and am momentarily confused by my surroundings until I remember that my dorm room has been rained on by the sprinklers and I'm at the hotel down the street. And I'm sleeping next to the guy I've been lusting after for weeks.

I hustle to the bathroom and close the door, then feel around for the light switch, blinking against the horrible brightness as my eyes struggle to adjust. I lock the door, gather up the giant hoodie, and nearly end up sitting in the toilet because the seat is up. "Fucking dudes and their noodles," I gripe.

I flip it down, and it hits the porcelain with a thwack. I'm too desperate to care if I wake up my roommate. I unleash a waterfall and groan at the relief. Once I'm done, I flush, wash my hands, and check to see if my clothes are dry. My pants are still damp, but my shirt and undies are dry. I fold the shirt and tuck my underwear between them but leave them on the vanity for morning.

I flick off the light before I leave the bathroom and wait a good thirty seconds for my eyes to readjust to the darkness before I open the door. I don't make it three steps before a huge looming figure appears in front of me.

Self-preservation mode is instantly activated. I grab the thick, well-muscled arm and come in low with my right shoulder, flipping the huge figure over my back.

It isn't until Chase lands on the floor with a groan and a thud that makes the whole room shake, that I realize my mistake.

CHAPTER 6

CHASE

One second I'm standing in the middle of the hotel room, waiting for the bathroom to be free, the next a shoulder is crammed into my stomach and I find myself flying through the air. And hitting the floor with enough force to knock the wind out of me.

"What the fuck," I groan.

The bedside light comes on.

"Shit. Sorry. You scared the crap out of me!" Cameron rushes across the room. Her hair is a wild mess, her eyes are wide, and she looks ridiculous in the massive hoodie that looks like it was made for a giant.

"Why the fuck did you do that?" I'm still lying on the floor, mostly because I'm trying to recover. I'm also processing what just happened. Weird little Cameron has suddenly turned into weird, fuckhot Cameron. There's literally nothing to her and she just flipped me over her shoulder. I'm six-four and two hundred pounds. There's nothing quite as sexy as a tiny woman who can kick ass.

"It was a reflex. I didn't expect you to be looming!"

"Looming?"

"You were standing there, being huge and imposing, and it freaked me out and I just reacted."

I roll up to a sitting position. "Did you think some random dude appeared out of nowhere?"

"I'm sorry. You scared me. Are you okay? Did I hurt you?" Her arms pinwheel, the too-long sleeves of the hoodie flopping around.

I hold up a hand. "I'm okay."

She takes it as a sign that I want her assistance, shoves a sleeve up, and wraps her small hand around mine. The contact isn't unwelcome, but the jolt it sends through me is foreign. It happened the first time, too. Maybe she's a staticky person. I let her help pull me to my feet.

She tips her chin up. "I'm really sorry."

"Where'd you learn how to do that?" I straighten my shirt and run a hand through my hair, trying to be cool about the fact that she just laid me out and I'm kind of a lot turned on by it.

"My sister and I had to learn how to fight young because my dad wanted us to be able to defend ourselves. I had a black belt in karate by the time I was fifteen."

"That's fucking hot," I blurt.

Cameron blinks up at me, cheeks turning pink. "Uh, thanks?" She takes a step back. "You needed the bathroom?"

"Right. Yeah."

I leave her standing there and close the bathroom door, locking it behind me. As I relieve myself, I notice that her panties are no longer hanging on the shower rod. But her shirt is folded on the counter. Is she wearing those panties again? Why am I suddenly turned on by the fact that she wears underwear proclaiming her pussy is her precious? I also wonder how many guys, if any, have had access to her precious. What if she has a boyfriend? The hot feeling creeping up the back of my neck is weird, and I don't know what to do with it. I shouldn't be thinking about her panties like some kind of fucking creep. She probably wouldn't have agreed to stay in this room with me if she had a boyfriend. Or she would have mentioned him. Girls with partners do that so straight dudes know not to shoot their shot for no reason.

I shake it off, literally, wash my hands, and return to the bedroom. The bedside lamp is still on. Cameron waits until I'm lying down again before she asks, "Should I turn out the light now?"

"If you want." I turn on my side and push the pillow between our heads down so I can see her profile. I don't know how I missed how pretty she is. Her bottom lip is fuller than her top lip, pouty and suckable. I try not to think about what it would feel like to have those luscious lips wrapped around *my* precious. And fail. "So you have an older sister, huh?"

"Yeah. She's really fun. And super pretty. She makes friends everywhere she goes and everyone loves her. High school was kind of weird because she was basically famous for being hot." Her voice starts to pitch up the longer she talks.

"Did that make it hard?" If her sister looks anything like her, I believe the hotness factor. But I don't care about her sister. I just want to know the girl in front of me.

"She's outgoing and I'm more of an introvert. She's cool though. I kind of lived in her shadow, but also it meant that people were nicer to me because of her, and mostly left me alone. I definitely wouldn't repeat high school, but it could have been worse. Anyway…" She takes a deep breath. "Do you have any siblings?"

I tuck my arm under my cheek, getting more comfortable. "One older sister and a younger brother."

"Oooh. The middle child." She rolls toward me and folds her pillow in half, then punches it down like she's annoyed with it. "Do you feel misunderstood most of the time?"

"Nah, my sister's only a year older and my brother's a year younger so there wasn't a lot of room to be misunderstood." I shift, trying to get comfortable, but my ribs are sore. "What's your major? What classes do you have this semester?"

"Seriously?" Her eyebrows rise.

"Yeah, seriously. I thought I saw you in bio last week."

Her nose wrinkles. It's pretty freaking cute. "Yeah, you did."

So I'm right, she's the same girl. "You live in res, right?" Unless she was just visiting a friend when I saw her in the elevator.

Her cheeks flush. "Uh, yeah."

I rub my bicep. "Right. Cool. What floor?"

"You're like three doors down from me." She rolls onto her back.

"You're kidding, right?" That means we've been passing each other in the halls for two months.

"Nope."

"We must sit on opposite sides of the lecture theater in bio." That's the only explanation for not knowing her before now.

She scoffs. "You literally sat on me during the first week. Like you didn't even see me sitting there, and your ass was in my lap."

"Oh shit. That was you?" I remember that. We'd gone to our teammate Mac's off-campus house for lunch and a swim but ended up drinking too many beers. I'd been half in the bag and not in the best form for that class. I'd fallen asleep and my teammates left me there. I woke up when the next class arrived, and some disapproving guy told me I should probably check with my classmates for notes since he was doubtful I'd retained much with the way I was hard-core drooling. He wasn't wrong.

"Yup. That was me." She rolls over and flicks off the light. "I'm tired, so I'm gonna go back to sleep."

"I'm sorry I sat on you."

"It's fine."

"It's not really, though." I was probably an asshole to her. I'm pretty sure the guys had laughed when it happened. I'm pretty sure *I* laughed.

"I knocked the wind out of you, so we're even. Night."

My throat suddenly feels tight. I want to keep pushing, but clearly she's done with me. "Night."

She pulls her covers over her head. I lie here feeling like a bag of shit.

I try to relax, but my mind keeps churning. How fucking oblivious am I that I completely overlooked her until last week? How many times have I walked right by her? How many opportunities have I missed to walk with her to class? Every beat of my heart sounds like a bass drum right now.

Her flipping me over her shoulder and laying me out on the floor keeps playing over and over in my head. She gets hotter and hotter with every replay.

I hit that weird zone between half awake and half asleep, and reach the point where the replay starts to morph. Instead of having the wind knocked out of me, Cameron straddles my hips, wraps her small, delicate but lethal hands around my wrists, and pins me to the floor. She rolls that full, pouty bottom lip of hers between her teeth and leans in until her mouth is barely out of reach. My shirt disappears and her braid sweeps across my chest, tickling my skin. And then she slides her precious over my erection and I groan, loudly.

My eyes pop open. My fist is wrapped around my erection, and I was probably about to sleep jerk it. It's a weird, embarrassing habit I have. Cameron rustles around beside me. Did I groan aloud? I really fucking hope not.

I let go of my dick and will my erection to fuck off. I think of unappealing things. Like zombies and roadkill and losing hockey games. But none of it works. Especially when Cameron makes this little sound that's half moan, half sigh.

I lie there for fifteen minutes, but my hard-on isn't giving up. If I don't take care of my problem, there's a good chance I'll wake up with raging morning wood. It's better if I handle it now. I tuck the sensitive head into my waistband and quietly slide out of bed. It shouldn't take long with how freaking worked up I am.

CHAPTER 7
CAMMIE

The bathroom door closes with a quiet snick. A few seconds later, the water turns on. I have a pretty good idea about what's happening behind that door. I've been lying here, pretending to sleep while Chase rustled around beside me. And then he groaned my name.

Groaned it.

The sound was all deep and needy and desperate. There is no way I can fall asleep knowing he's probably whacking off. Possibly to thoughts of me. *Probably to thoughts of me*.

After being pummeled into the dirt when I realized that Chase has legitimately never even noticed me until last week even though he sat on me at the beginning of the semester, my almost nonexistent ego has grown three full sizes in the last five minutes. So what if fate and bad planning are what threw us together? He sure is noticing me now.

Maybe it's only because he's forced to be my roommate. But he has friends here. Teammates like Brody and Gage. Surely, he could have crashed in one of their rooms if he were completely opposed to being trapped with me tonight.

I roll onto my back and consider helping myself out while

Chase is doing the same in the bathroom. But the likelihood that I'll finish before he does is slim to none.

I don't want to be the wallflower who's so invisible I get sat on in class anymore. I don't want to be Essie's weird little sister. I want to be the hot warrior princess who can toss around a two-hundred-plus-pound hockey player. I can be forward. I can channel my inner Arwen, just like O said. I can go for what I want. Which is…what exactly?

To watch Chase get himself off? I conjure that image for a moment. Chase's big hand curved around what I imagine will be an equally big cock, stroking away. Based on the way everything below the waist starts pinging, I'm definitely down with at least watching if he is.

Decision made, I throw off the covers and pull the hoodie over my head, tossing it on the bed. I will not sit on the bench and twiddle my thumbs while Chase is getting himself off in the bathroom. The bow I tied on my university-issued pants comes undone with a quick tug and they immediately drop to the floor.

I cross the room and grab the door handle. But then I pause. I can't just bust in there. I'm about to knock when his muffled groan filters through the door.

"Ah, fuck. That's it." A low groan follows.

I knock softly. "Chase?"

"Fuck. Just give me a minute."

My mouth goes dry and my fingers twitch as I grip the doorknob. I can do this. I want to do this. I slowly, carefully, quietly turn the knob. Taking a deep breath, I open it a crack.

Chase has one hand planted on the vanity. The other grips his impressive cock. I was so right about the size. It matches the rest of him. His gaze shifts toward the door and when his eyes meet mine, I surprise myself by not issuing an apology, slamming the door shut, and making a hasty retreat under the covers.

Instead, I lick my lips and channel my inner seductress, which I was unaware existed at all until this very moment. "Please don't stop."

Chase's eyes flare as his cheeks turn pink. But he doesn't make a move to tuck himself back into his pajama pants, which I take as a green light. He seems confused, but also intrigued.

My eyes drop as he gives his cock a tentative stroke. I push the door open, my gaze raking over him greedily. He's just so fucking beautiful. Broad shoulders, defined biceps, tight forearms, thick chest, and rolling abs. His pajama pants have been pushed down so one deliciously round globe of tight ass is on display.

His thumb smooths over the head as he drags his fist back down. My entire body heats, a flush working its way from the tip of my toes to the top of my head.

I lean casually against the doorframe and finger the bottom of my shirt. "If you're getting off, so am I."

He blinks twice, licks his bottom lip, and nods. "Yeah. Yes. That…I want that."

His eagerness bolsters my confidence. I slowly drag the hem of the stupidly oversized shirt up, revealing bare thighs, but stop when I reach the apex of them. I slide a single finger between my folds and circle my clit.

Chase's rhythm falters, eyes flipping between my face and where my finger dips between my thighs. He pats the top of the vanity. "You should sit up here. It'll be better for you."

As I hop up on the cold marble, I notice that my underwear is no longer tucked under my shirt. Interesting. I hike the shirt up, gathering it at my waist and tying a knot so it doesn't get in the way. I can't believe I'm about to have a mutual masturbation session. With the hot hockey player I've been lusting after for the past two months. This better not be a fever dream.

Chase seems to stop breathing as I part my thighs and reveal myself.

"Oh my fucking God," he groans.

My ego inflates a little more. *I turn Chase on. Me.* Despite how wet I already am, I slip my index finger between my lips.

Chase's gaze turns molten as I lower my hand between my thighs and gently circle my clit.

"Fuck. Wait." He steps closer, chest heaving. His eyes are wild as they move from my face to where my finger presses against my hot button, paralyzed with fear and uncertainty. Did I get this all wrong? Misread the signs?

"I want to make you come." He rolls his shoulders back. "If you want me to, that is."

I cock my head, considering my words carefully. I go with the most brazen, blush-inducing phrase I've ever uttered to a guy I want to get with. "You want to touch my precious?" Except I meant to say *pussy*, but it's too late to take it back.

"Fuck. Yes." His grip on his cock tightens and his eyes fall closed as he exhales in a rush. When they open again, they're an inferno of lust. "Please say that again."

His reaction spurs me on. I slip my finger lower, circling my entrance. "Do you want to finger-fuck my precious, Chase?"

"Absolutely, Cameron." He nods vigorously. "I one million percent want to finger-fuck your precious." He moves to stand between my thighs. "Can I kiss you first, though?"

"Okay."

He releases his cock and cups my face between his warm palms. I push away the thought his penis hand is now resting against the side of my neck. His expression is intense as he leans in. He's tentative at first, lips brushing gently over mine.

When I lick his top lip, he groans and tips his head, parting for me. Our tongues meet and tangle. I trail my fingers over the glorious dips and planes of his cut body. I'm making out with a hockey player. A really hot, well-endowed hockey player. This is a check mark on my bucket list.

I half expect him to be aggressive, but he's completely the opposite. He's soft, gentle, and sweet, our tongues brushing and exploring. As far as first kisses go, this is an award winner.

While we make out, I follow the line bisecting his abs past his navel. My fingertips brush the satin-smooth skin of his erection, causing him to groan and his fingers to tighten in my hair.

He breaks the kiss, his breath leaving him on a ragged pant as my fingers curve around his length. I feel like a damn goddess as his gaze drops.

"Ah fuck, that feels so good, Cameron."

"Cammie, I go by Cammie."

"Cammie, your hand is fucking bliss," he declares.

Both of our gazes drop as I continue to stroke him, thumb sweeping over the head when I reach the crown.

His hand settles on my knee and slowly trails up. My breath catches as his fingertips brush my inner thigh. I'm still stroking him as he dips between my legs and skims my clit. He makes another needy noise as he drags his finger through my slit and circles my entrance.

Normally, reciprocal masturbation is fraught with awkwardness, especially with someone new, but this is just…hot. His mouth drops open, and his tongue peeks out as he eases a single finger inside me. I moan—at the look of desire on his gorgeous face, at the feel of his finger curling against that sensitive place inside me, at the heat of his cock in my hand.

His gaze lifts and a slow smile spreads across his very kissable lips. "Such a pretty precious."

I wrap my free hand around the back of his neck and drag his mouth back to mine. This kiss isn't soft and sweet like the first one. It's fraught with lust and need. We keep kissing and touching. My hand moving over his cock in time with the pump and curl of his finger inside me. He adds a second, stretching me, filling me. We moan and pant, shift and grip and caress.

I break the kiss long enough to say, "One more finger, please."

"You're so tight, though. You're sure?"

"My pussy can handle it," I pant.

"Fuck, I love that," he groans.

We both watch as his fingers slide out and he adds a third,

pushing back in slowly. I let go of his hair, lick my index finger, and rub circles on my clit.

"That's so fucking sexy. You're so fucking sexy, Cammie," Chase groans.

"So are you," I murmur. "I'm getting close."

"Yeah?" His eyes flare with excitement. "Tell me what you need so I can get you there."

"Just keep doing what you're doing." I want this so badly. To come while he's touching me, to have this experience as fodder for my self-gratification sessions. To be the girl who isn't afraid to take what she wants.

He curls his fingers. "Like this?"

"That's it. Right there. That's the spot." I keep stroking him and my clit while he rubs the spot from the inside. "Such a good boy," I murmur.

I bite my lip, because I didn't mean to say that last part aloud.

His smile turns devilish. "You gonna come all over my fingers, like a good girl, Cammie?"

And that's it. I'm done for. I moan his name, long and loud as pleasure pulses through me in glorious waves. For a moment I lose my rhythm, too caught up in the sensation washing through me. But as soon as I have control over my limbs again, I tighten my grip and stroke him in earnest.

He grips the edge of the vanity, hips jerking as he angles his erection toward the sink and comes all over the marble.

I wait for the awkwardness to hit post-orgasm, or for him to get all weird about it, but he drops his forehead to my shoulder and turns until his nose brushes my neck and his lips follow. "That was so much fun."

I laugh. "It absolutely was."

"Wanna cuddle and try to get a little more sleep?"

"I could be persuaded."

CHAPTER 8

CHASE

I wake to Cammie draped across my body. Her leg is thrown over mine, small hand resting on my chest, pillow tucked into the crook of my arm where her head rests. Her long lashes fan across her cheek, her full lips are parted, and every so often she makes a little humming sound. She's so fucking beautiful. I seriously can't believe she didn't enter my orbit albeit fleetingly until last night. I've been so caught up in my own shit.

My phone buzzes on the nightstand. I reach for it, unsure of the time. The clock flashes four thirteen, but there's light peeking through the narrow gap in the curtains.

I have messages from the guys and new ones from the university app. Apparently classes and practice are canceled today on account of the storm. Several buildings are without power. While I was getting a bathroom handy, we had a near tornado rip through campus, followed by torrential rain and a hailstorm. Currently, conditions are windy and icy, and the message is to avoid going out for any reason other than emergencies.

Which means I have a whole day with Cammie. Maybe we'll get each other off again. More than once. Corresponding body parts perk up at the prospect. I wish I could reach my backpack so I could pop a mint.

Cammie stretches and her hand slides over my chest, fingers brushing my nipple. As she toys with it, her lips pucker, and her brows furrow. Eventually one lid cracks, then the other. Her eyes dart around and lift to my face. Assessing. Processing.

When she starts to lift her hand, I cover it with mine. She frowns and uses her other hand to pinch herself. "Ow." Her tongue drags across her full bottom lip. "Did I have a fever dream last night, or did you put your fingers in my pussy?"

"I absolutely did that. And you came on them." I would do it a thousand times over just to watch her unravel for me.

She pokes her cheek with her tongue. "And I gave you a handy?"

"Yeah. It was fucking amazing. I would love to do it again. The putting my fingers in your precious and you touching my… me."

"Cool." Her lips push out in a semi-pensive pout. "I need to pee." She throws the covers off and rolls out of bed. She hikes the shirt she's wearing up as she pads across the floor, giving me a peek of cheek as she scratches the back of her thigh.

I quickly roll out of bed and chew two mints to get rid of my morning breath. My eyes water, so I chug from the bottle on the nightstand, but it only makes the burning worse. I hop back into bed and try to cop a casual pose. Should I be on my side or like just propped up on my back? But when she returns from the bathroom she's fully dressed in her clothes from yesterday.

"I should probably get ready for class. What time is it even?"

I check my phone. "It's eight thirty. But classes are canceled because of the storm." I motion to the window, which I haven't checked since I've been awake. The school news feed makes it sound bad.

She crosses the room in her black jeans and a T-shirt. I know what she's hiding under there, and I'm a fan. She parts the curtains and retracts the blackout blinds.

"Holy shit. You should check this out."

I tuck my half hard-on into the waistband of my boxer briefs and reluctantly get out of bed. "Holy shit is right." Tree branches litter the parking lot and the boulevard, and a small tree has toppled over completely. Most of the cars in the lot have dents in the hoods and roofs. There must be an inch of half-melted hail littering the ground. It's a mess out there.

"I guess we're stuck here for the time being," Cammie muses.

Would it be weird if I wrapped my arms around her? Probably. "Looks that way." My stomach makes an awful gurgling sound.

She arches her brow. "I bet you need to feed that beast frequently."

I pat my abs. "Yeah. I usually don't go more than a few hours without a meal."

My phone buzzes from the nightstand several times.

"Looks like someone really needs you," Cammie observes.

"It's probably the guys." I grab it. I'm right. They're talking about food. It's a common occurrence. "You wanna grab breakfast with me and a few of my teammates? I can introduce you. There's a buffet in the hotel restaurant."

"Oh, uh." Cammie fingers the end of her ponytail. It's kinky from the braid she had it in last night. "I'm good. I've got a few granola bars in my bag, and there's a coffee maker in the room."

"We get to eat free. And it's a buffet." I love buffets. Endless food options and no limits.

"You go ahead. I have some work I need to do." She smiles and pats my stomach when it rumbles again. "Seriously. You should eat."

"We'll hang out after?"

"Yeah. Sounds good." She busies herself with setting up the coffee maker while I throw on my clothes.

"You want me to bring you anything back?"

"If they have any nice fruit, I'd take something for later, thanks." She pulls books and her laptop out of her bag.

"No problem." I pull on the pajama pants and T-shirt, grab the keycard, shove my feet into my shoes, and head up to Gage and Brody's room.

They've already flipped the security latch so I can let myself in.

Brody is sitting on his bed with his phone in his hand, drinking coffee and eating cookies. Gage is styling his hair.

"How was last night with the weird girl?" Gage asks.

"Uh. She's actually not that weird. I just shocked her when I came barging into the room." I rub the back of my neck, thinking about the way she flipped me over her shoulder like a ninja.

Brody's eyes flare. "Dude. What the fuck happened last night?"

"Huh?"

"You have the face," Brody says.

"The face?" I run a hand down mine.

"Yeah. The I-got-lucky face," Brody clarifies.

"Did you fuck her?" Gage asks.

"No, man. I didn't… We didn't have sex." But I would definitely have sex with her if she wanted to. Hands fucking down.

"But something happened," Brody presses.

"Yeah. We uh…we made out. But uh…this isn't like a party hookup."

"Because you were sober?" Gage asks.

"No. I mean, yeah, I was sober, and she was sober, but I think…I think I actually like her. Like yes, I want to get naked with her and just—" I stop before I admit more than I want, but based on their expressions, I'm already over the line. "Like I want to hang out with her while also fully clothed…and get to know her better." I prop my fists on my hips. "I'd rather be in the room with her right now than here with you guys."

"Because you want to fuck her," Gage says. His mind has one well-worn track.

"Yes, but even if she doesn't want to fuck, I would still want to hang out with her." I'd actually be sad if she didn't want to at least make out again, though. Those lips will haunt my dreams for the rest of my life.

"So you like her," Brody states.

"Yes." I rub the back of my neck. "I do. Fuck. Shit. How do I handle this?"

Gage shrugs and Brody rolls his eyes.

"Seriously. I'm used to girls throwing themselves at me because I play hockey and they want a piece of me. And most of the time I'm just happy to have someone's much softer body parts wrapped around my cock."

"Fuck yeah, man." Gage holds out his hand for a fist bump.

I tap his fist, but only because he won't let up unless I do.

"But this is different. Yes, I want her prec—soft parts wrapped around my cock. One hundred percent. But I actually wanted her to come down for breakfast so you could meet her."

"So why isn't she here?"

"She had some work to do."

"So why don't you bring her breakfast so you can hang out and eat together and you can get to know each other," Brody suggests like the genius he is. With two older brothers, he's well versed in the whole witnessing relationships thing. And Tristan is engaged, which is more than I can say for my older sister who hasn't dated anyone since middle school.

"Is it Human Physiology homework? Because if it is you could make it totally hands on," Gage suggests. "Just like I wish I could with my tutor but can't if I don't want to end up failing the course."

"Remember you said that the next time you're plotting to seduce her," Brody says, then turns to me. "If you actually like her, I suggest holding off on sex, but totally up to you."

"Yeah, good call. I'm going to grab some food and bring it back to the room."

Brody shoves the last cookie into his face and hops off the bed. "We'll come down with you. I'm starving."

We pile into the elevator. I end up sitting at a table for a bit with a bunch of my teammates and load up on food so I'm not shoveling it into my face when I get back up to the room. The girl who keeps inviting me and my teammates to keg parties shows up looking like she had a rough night.

"Hey, Chase! Hey, Brodes and Gage!"

I push my chair back and stand. "You want a seat?"

She hugs me. "That is so sweet! You're just so sweet, Chase!"

Literally everything she says ends with an exclamation point.

Brody shoots me a death glare, but Gage doesn't seem put off by her overly enthusiastic personality.

"I'm gonna grab some stuff." I point to the buffet. I load up two plates with a little of everything since I'm not sure what she likes. I also nab a few granola bars since they have plenty of those. Once I'm stocked, I head for the elevators.

Keg Party girl is busy hanging off Gage's arm, so she doesn't notice me leaving. On the way up to the room, I give myself a pep talk. "You got this, man. You can just hang out, feed her, talk. And then maybe if things go well, you'll get to touch her again." I exhale a long breath and try to push away the image of my fingers buried in all that soft wetness. But the way she looked, and the sound of my name tumbling from her lips when she came is tough to shove back in a box. "One step at a time. Food and conversation. You know how to eat and talk. You get eighties in all your courses. You're not an intellectual slouch. You're more than just a hockey player with a nice face." The elevator doors slide open.

Two girls I vaguely recognize say hi. I mutter hi back and head down the hall to my room. My phone goes off with a text from Gage.

GAGE

She's into you. You're into her. You got this, man. Just have fun. You're Chase fucking Lovett.

I swipe the key over the sensor and throw open the door a little too hard. “Hey, Cammie! I brought you breakfast in bed!”

I round the corner as she slams her laptop closed. Her eyes are wide, and her face is red. “Hey. Hi. Uh, I didn’t expect you to be back so soon.”

“What’s this about?” I make a circle motion around my face.

“What’s what about?” She runs her hands up and down her thighs.

“You’re all shifty.” I set the tray down on the bed. “Were you watching porn or something?” I mean it as a joke, and for the words not to come out all low and gravelly.

CHAPTER 9

CAMMIE

"Cammie?" Chase tips his head.

Having his attention on me is overwhelming and incredibly flattering. But he asked a question, and I have yet to answer him.

"I was writing my fic." Oh my God, I just told him I write fanfic. I never tell anyone.

"Why are you flushed?"

"Let me rephrase that. I was writing high-spice romance," I say, a little haughtily.

"High-spice romance?" Chase parrots.

"I should have just said I was working on an assignment." It's what I should be doing. "Thanks for bringing all of this stuff back for me." I choose a blueberry muffin and peel off the wrapper so I have something to do with my hands and a place for my eyes to be that isn't on Chase.

"No problem." He rounds the bed and drops down beside me.

"This is to share, right?" I'm famished but there's no way I can eat all of it. Especially not with all the butterflies bopping around in my stomach.

"I had some while I was down at the buffet. You eat what you want, and I'll clean up the leftovers."

"I bet you could literally eat all day long and never get full," I muse.

"It's a rare hour when I'm not hungry." He adjusts the pillows. "I want to know more about this spicy romance stuff."

I pull the hood over my head to hide my face. "It'd be better if you pretend I didn't say that out loud."

"Now I definitely need to know more." He tugs the hood back down and skims my cheek with his fingers. "Are you embarrassed?"

I sigh. "No. Yes. No. You're going to think I'm weird."

"You are weird. But I like your weird."

I side-eye him. "I actually didn't think you would come back."

He frowns. "What do you mean?"

I roll my eyes to the ceiling. "I figured you'd find your friends and they'd find more friends and you'd end up hanging out and we'd get called back to the dorms and that would be that."

He runs a hand through his hair, eyes darting to the side. "Is that what you wanted to happen?" He sounds so…hurt, almost?

"No, but last night, emotions were running pretty high and things happened, and I don't want you to feel like you have to hang out with me because of that." This is one of my biggest personal issues. In high school, sometimes I'd be invited to things, but often it was in the hopes that I'd bring my sister along. These days I'm mostly the silent observer no one notices, but I have these moments, like last night and now, where I step out of the box and go with the bluntest honesty ever.

"I'm not hanging out with you because I feel obligated. I'm hanging out with you because I like you. You're fucking beautiful, you're cool as shit, you tell it like it is, and you're a little dirty. Which I'm super down with, by the way. Not that I expect more of what happened last night, but just know my hands are one hundred percent committed to bringing you pleasure whenever you want it."

"Last night was fun." I'm not telling him I like him too, even though I do. Every cisgendered female in our dorm is lusting after him, just like me. He needs zero in the way of an ego boost.

"So much fun." He taps my laptop. "Now back to this spicy romance business. I need to know more about it."

I sigh. "I write *Lord of the Rings* fanfic."

"You mean those movies with the hobbits and stuff?" he asks.

"They were books before they were movies," I point out.

"Right. Yeah. They're super long, the books and the movies. I mostly listen to audiobooks when I have to read novels."

"It's still reading, just with your ears." Plus, it can really bring the story to life with the right narrators. And don't get me started on the immersive graphic audio. That's a movie in your mind. I turn every hero into Aragorn.

"So back to this fanfic. I want to know more."

I roll my eyes to the ceiling. Am I really going to admit this? "I write Arwen, Legolas, and Aragorn stories."

"I don't know what that means," Chase says.

"Where the three of them end up together."

"Together as in…"

"Bed. Or wherever, but they get naked with each other."

Chase blinks at me. "Like a threesome?"

"Yeah." I wait for him to start laughing.

"One girl, two guys?" he clarifies.

"Yes."

His brows pull together and his gaze narrows. "Is that like… a thing for you?"

I can't figure out his expression. "In fanfic, yes."

His eyes narrow further. "What about in real life?"

My brows shoot up. "Uh, I mean, I guess if Aragorn and Legolas were real people I would jump into that scenario, but mostly I don't like my attention on more than one person at a time."

His shoulders come down from his ears. "Okay, good. That's good."

I shove his shoulder. "Oh my God. Were you jealous for a hot second?"

"Pfft. No." He runs his hand through his hair and side-eyes me. "Yeah, actually."

"You really do like me." I'm mystified as to how this happened, but also my ego is really enjoying this. Chase Lovett, who should be way out of my league, *is into me*.

"Yeah. I told you that." He rests his head on my knee. "Can I read some of your threesome fanfic?"

"It's really smutty."

"I love smutty."

"You can't laugh."

"I promise not to laugh." He crosses his heart and gives me puppy-dog eyes.

I can't believe I'm doing this. I've mentioned in passing to my real-life university friend Tally that I write fanfic, but she doesn't know my pen name, or what kind I write. Yet here I am, showing this guy who fingerbanged me, my private, dirty thoughts. I flip open my laptop and scroll to the top of the page.

I set the scene for him. "Legolas and Arwen just returned from a quest to get supplies, and Aragorn is waiting for them with a hot bath."

"Cool." Chase scoots closer so his upper body is pressed against my crossed leg. He props his cheek on his fist. His lips move while he reads, but he doesn't make any sound, eyes darting back and forth.

When he reaches the bottom of the page, he scrolls up. "I thought you said this was like word porn. There's like an actual story and stakes."

My cheeks are on fire. "Well yeah, it can't be all smut, all the time. But most chapters start out with some light plot and then get to the fun stuff."

"Got it. This is really good. Like I don't read much aside from my textbooks, and the occasional audiobook, but the descriptions are great, and I feel like I'm in their house with them."

"Really?"

"Yeah. Really." He smiles up at me. "Now stop talking, I want to know what happens next."

He keeps scrolling and reading, his lips moving, eyebrows popping every so often. When his face starts to turn red, I can tell he's getting to the bath scene. "Damn," he mutters, scrolling so quickly he has to backtrack. "This is fucking hot, Cammie."

"Thanks." I pull the neck of my hoodie up to my eyeballs, so I can read along with him, but also so I can hide.

"Oh yeah, that's…" He shifts around. "'My hands follow the soapy water as it cascades over her luscious bare breasts. Legolas covers one stiff peak with his full lips, as his other hand dips below the water.'"

I slap a palm over Chase's mouth. "Do not read aloud."

He mumbles something from behind my palm.

I drop my hand and give him my best annoyed face.

He blinks up at me with wide, imploring eyes. "Will you read it to me?"

"No. That's—I'm not reading it to you."

"Pretty please? I'll do anything you want. Literally anything. Strip naked and run down the hall. Wear a tutu to class. Sing in the middle of the quad."

I bite back a smile. "Read it silently or you don't read at all. Those are your options."

"Fine." He sighs, but he goes back to scrolling while I eat the yogurt parfait he brought me.

When he reaches the end, he frowns. "Where's the next chapter?"

"I was just starting it when you came back with breakfast." I lick the spoon clean and set the empty container aside.

Chase sits up, eyes wide. "But I want to know what happens next! They get out of the bath and towel Arwen off and then what?"

"I think it's pretty obvious what happens next." It doesn't take a rocket scientist to figure out that they end up in bed.

"Yeah, but I want to read about it. You should keep writing." He tries to move my hands to the keyboard.

"I can't write with you reading over my shoulder."

"Why not?"

"Because it's weird."

He arches a brow.

I arch one back.

"Fine, why don't you tell me what's supposed to happen next instead." He props his elbows on his knees and rests his chin on them.

"They take it to the bedroom and fuck," I deadpan.

He gives me an unimpressed look. "What about the foreplay? There must be foreplay. All they did was soap each other up in the bath." He backtracks. "Which was hot for sure, but what about the fingerbangs and handies?"

I roll my eyes. "Obviously that's part of what happens next."

"What else is part of what happens next?"

"Probably some oral," I mutter.

"Do Legolas and Aragorn take turns eating Arwen out?" Chase tries to surreptitiously move his dick around in his pants. His eyes are lit up with excitement and lust. "Does Arwen blow them while they tongue-fuck her?"

"Sure." The scene has been playing out in my head for a week, I just haven't had time to put it down.

"Come on, Cammie. I need details. What about positions? Whose face does Arwen sit on first? This guy needs to know." He pokes himself in the chest.

"Aragorn's face. She would sit on his face first."

"Because he didn't get to go on the quest and he's missed her precious the most while Legolas didn't have to share her for however long they were gone," Chase muses.

"Basically, yeah."

"But where's Legolas? Is he feeling left out?" Chase seems legitimately concerned about Legolas's whereabouts.

"He's on the bed, too." In my head, I picture Chase stretched out on the very bed we're sitting on, naked, with Arwen's (my) knees on either side of his head, in position for a sixty-niner, but with a lighter-haired Chase number two straddling Chase number one's thighs, so Arwen (I) has easy access to both of their cocks.

"I have an idea," Chase says.

I bite the inside of my cheek.

"Now you can tell me to fuck the hell off if you want, but what if we acted out the scene? For research purposes, minus Legolas, because it's just you and me." His tongue drags across his bottom lip.

"You want to eat me out?" Based on the tingles below the waist, my pussy really likes this idea.

"I'd fucking love to eat you out." He nods vigorously. "Like so much."

"And you'd also like me to blow you, while you tongue-fuck me." Obviously I need to clarify the parameters.

"Only if you want to reciprocate." He swallows thickly and nods once. "But yes, please."

I've never sixty-nined before, so this will be something new for me. "Okay."

"Seriously?" He seems shocked.

I shrug, trying to act nonchalant when really I'm freaking out. Chase Lovett wants to put his face between my legs. It's like two bucket list items at the same time. "Yeah. Why not?"

He hops off the bed. "Let me just move all this stuff." He grabs the tray of food.

"I need a minute to freshen up."

"Sure. You go ahead. I'll manage this stuff." He sets the food on the coffee table and moves my laptop to the desk on the other side of the room.

I disappear into the bathroom and lock the door. I wish I had my phone so I could text Tally about this. Or even my sister? No. Not my sister. Knowing her, she'd fight her way through the apocalypse outside to throw me a fucking party.

I grip the countertop and stare at my reflection in the mirror. "You can put Chase Lovett's huge penis in your mouth while he licks your pussy." She clenches at her mention. "Channel your inner dirty Arwen, Cammie. You can do this."

I wet a washcloth and soap it up, giving my important parts a little bath, then brush my teeth and hair before I leave the safety of the bathroom. Chase is standing in the middle of the room in only his boxer briefs. He really is a glorious specimen of man-boy. He meets me in the middle of the room.

He lifts his hand and his fingers trail gently down my cheek. "If you change your mind at any time, Cammie, just tell me and we'll stop, okay?"

"Okay." I settle my palms on his broad chest and slide them over his shoulders, linking my fingers behind his neck.

"Can I kiss you now?"

"On my face lips?"

He grins. "Seems like the most reasonable place to start."

"Okay, then."

I tip my chin up and close my eyes as he tips his down. I'm so nervous, and excited. I can't believe I get to experience this first with the literal guy of my dreams.

His lips brush over mine, softly, sweetly. One hand slides into my hair, cupping the back of my head, his other winds around my waist, pulling me against him. He's all hard lines and tight muscles and smooth skin. And the way he kisses me, like I'm something to be savored, makes my knees weak.

Eventually he pulls back, takes my hand, and guides me to the end of the bed. He fingers the sleeve that reaches my elbow. "Can I take some of this stuff off?"

"Probably a good idea."

He carefully removes my shirt, brushing my hair over my shoulder after he drops it on the floor. I'm so thankful I didn't wear a bra last night. His eyes lock on my boobs and he makes a deep sound in the back of his throat.

Chase drops to his knees. He's an exceptionally tall guy, and I'm slightly below average height so his face is almost at boob level.

He tips his head back to look at me. "Can I touch your tatas?"

"Only if you never call them tatas again."

"Never again." He inhales deeply and raises his hands but stops just shy of cupping my breasts. He touches his cheek first. "Temperature check. Cold hands are the worst."

"That's the truth."

He gently curves his huge palms around them. Then he does that thing that guys always seem compelled to do. He jiggles them a little and follows it up by brushing his thumbs over my nipples. "Fuck, your tits."

"It's probably more gratifying for you than me."

His eyes shoot to mine. "I didn't mean that literally, just that they're amazing."

"Thanks. I'm pretty attached to them." Why am I making bad jokes when he's holding my boobs and saying nice things about them?

His tongue drags across his bottom lip. "Can I kiss them?"

"Sure. Go ahead."

"Thanks." He kisses the swell first, eyes still on my face. And then he gently brushes his lips back and forth over the tight peak.

I run my fingers through his hair, enthralled and completely overwhelmed by how incredible it is to have this giant, hot hockey player on his knees in front of me, being gentle when his job on the ice is the opposite. His eyes flutter shut, and his tongue peeks out to tease the peak before his lips close over it. Warm, and wet, and soft.

All my needy body parts respond, my stomach tightening, heat flooding my center. Chase devotes the same attention to the other nipple. And then he pushes to his feet, hands sliding around to cup my ass as he lifts me off the floor like I weigh nothing.

I shriek and grip his shoulders as he spins around and lays me on the bed, then shifts to the right, turning us on our sides.

"That was exceptionally graceful," I note.

"Thanks." He kisses me again, hand still on my boob. It moves down my stomach, and he pops the button on my jeans. "This is still okay?"

"Definitely. Yes. No pants will make eating me out a lot easier."

"Truth." He drags the zipper down.

I get impatient and shove my pants and underwear over my hips, gracelessly kicking them off. Chase's hand trails down my stomach. He doesn't immediately go for the hot button and rub it like he's expecting a genie to appear. Instead, he slides his hand between my thighs and cups me. "I'm so fucking excited to get real personal with your precious."

I laugh and he smiles.

"Should we try out the scene you were writing? For research purposes, of course." His eyes are alight with carnal desire.

"Sure. Yeah. Okay." This is actually happening. I'm going to sit on Chase's face. On purpose.

He rolls onto his back and shoves his boxers down his muscular thighs. They're ridiculous. His erection springs free, bobbing once before it smacks against his stomach.

He lies on his back and adjusts the pillow, then beckons me closer. "Bring that precious over here."

"You don't have to keep calling it that."

"Yeah, I do. It's part of the scene. Bring it hither."

"Please never say *hither* again."

"For the love of God, Cammie, put a desperate man out of his fucking misery, and sit on my face."

Well, when he puts it that way… "Sir, yes, sir." I straddle his head, feeling all kinds of exceptionally awkward as I try to keep my balance and not accidentally suffocate him with my vagina.

I brace my weight on one hand and grip his erection in my other. He groans and kneads my ass. Then gives the right cheek a smack.

I startle and look down at him through my spread legs. His eyes are wide.

"Sorry. So sorry. Just…your ass is great, and I didn't think."

"It's okay."

He bites the back of my thigh, not hard, but enough to stoke the fire working its way through my body. I give his cock a few gentle strokes. I remind myself that I can fit an entire popsicle in my mouth, and this isn't massively different apart from girth.

I start by kissing the tip. Chase wriggles around under me and tries to pull my vagina closer to his face. When he strokes me with his tongue, my bracing arm almost gives out. I give the head of his cock the ice cream cone treatment, but then something presses against my opening and his tongue finds my clit and I moan.

Chase makes an approving noise and keeps up with the licking. I try to bob on his erection, but mostly I'm just holding it in my mouth and moaning. And then I feel something press against the back door.

I pop off. "Chase?"

"Okay, so I think in theory this is a fun position, but I feel like it requires a lot of multitasking and I'm not great at that, so maybe I can just focus on you for a while and you can focus on me later, if you want to," Chase says.

I roll off him and am so thankful I don't knee him in the face. "Or I could focus on you now."

He narrows his eyes and shakes his head. "You come first."

He's a rare gem. "If you insist."

"I do." He sits up in a rush, grabs me by the waist, and flips me onto my back. And then he peppers kisses down my body. His gaze lifts as he settles between my thighs, shoulders nudging them wider. He turns his head and presses his lips to the inside of my thigh. "This is so much better." He moves to the inside of the other thigh and drops wet kisses all over my sex before he finally licks a path from my entrance to my clit.

"So fucking good," he mumbles against my hot skin.

We both groan, and I bite my lip and slap a hand over my mouth.

"Oh, hell no." Chase grabs my hand and pulls it away from my face. "Those moans are mine and I want to hear every last one of them."

He dives back in, alternating soft strokes of tongue with toe-curling suction. I slide my hands into his hair and adjust the pillow so I can watch. I still can't believe he's eating me out. Deep, primal growls and groans hum across my clit every time I sigh or moan or whimper, which I do often because *oh my God,* his mouth is magical. I wish this experience could last forever. I roll my hips as sensation builds and spirals.

"I'm so close," I mutter, just in case his tongue is getting tired and he needs some encouragement to keep going.

He adjusts his position, cheek resting against the inside of my thigh as he slides two fingers inside me and curls. It sends me careening into sensation overload. I moan his name, and my legs shake violently as everything below the waist clenches. Waves of pleasure wash over me, and a blanket of sheer bliss consumes me.

He keeps lapping at me until I pull roughly on his hair. "Too sensitive. Precious needs a break."

He lifts his head and swipes at his mouth with the back of his hand. "Did I do good?"

"So good. Better than good. You win the MVPL award for Most Valuable Pussy Licker."

He prowls up my body, dropping kisses as he goes, pausing to say hi to my sensitive nipples on the way. "I'd wear that shirt." He brushes his lips over mine.

I can smell myself all over his face and I kind of love it. "I'd love to return the favor, but I don't know if I can move more than my mouth at the moment."

One eyebrow tips up and his smile is downright devilish. "I could make it easier for you."

"Okay."

He shifts and straddles my chest, his huge body looming over me as he rises and tucks his knees tightly on either side of my ribs. His impressive erection bobs above me.

Chase gently but firmly slides his fingers into my hair and cups my head in his palms. "I'd like to fuck your mouth, please," he grinds out.

My vagina clenches all over again at the deliciously dark look on his gorgeous face. "I'd like that, too."

I part my lips and grip the shaft, helping guide his cock inside my mouth.

"No hands, Cammie."

I settle them on his thighs, halfway to another orgasm just from that one command. And as promised, Chase absolutely makes it easier for me. He holds my head and fucks my mouth with slow, long strokes that pick up speed as I adjust to his size. All I have to do is slurp and hum and suck and moan.

He warns me that he's about to come and I grab hold of his rock-solid ass and try—but mostly fail—to deep-throat him.

But I swallow like a champ.

CHAPTER 10

CAMMIE

"That was fucking awesome. You're fucking awesome." Chase is lying beside me, wearing a huge smile and nothing else.

"Thanks, so are you." I can't believe he just fucked my face. And I loved it.

I'm totally writing this experience into my story.

I want to share this with O, but she's a high school senior. Although, she reads all my dirty *LotR* fanfic, so this isn't much different. But I could tell Tally when I see her in English later this week. *What is this life I'm suddenly living*?

Chase's phone buzzes from somewhere in the room. It happened a bunch of times during our oral session, and throughout the night. I guess that's what it's like to be popular. Everyone always wants your attention. He rolls off the bed and searches the floor for his pants. He should never wear clothes. His body is unreal.

"Some of the guys are hanging out in the restaurant downstairs," he announces.

"You should go chill with them." And I'll stay up here and continue writing my fanfic. Even though I should really put some words down on my creative writing submission.

He tosses his phone onto the bed and lithely jumps on top of me, covering me like a blanket. "Come down with me. I want you to meet my friends."

"I should finish my chapter so you have something to read later."

"You don't want to meet my friends?" He looks hurt by the prospect.

I bite the inside of my cheek. I see him and his friends in the common room and on campus all the time. They're the cool jocks and I'm the weird fanfic-writing nerd.

"Please? Just come hang out for a bit." He bats his lashes. "I'll eat your precious again when we come back up here."

"Way to sell it." I run my fingers through his hair, trying to tame the mess I made.

"Is that a yes?"

"Sure. Yeah. I'll come down with you. I could use a cold caffeinated beverage right about now, anyway."

"Awesome! I'll let them know we'll be down in a few."

He rolls off the bed and gathers our clothes from the floor, tossing mine at me. It takes me three times as long to get dressed and I stop in the bathroom to fix my hair and brush my teeth. My lips are puffy thanks to the face fuck.

Once we're both dressed, I follow Chase into the hall. "Gage can come across as cocky at first, but he's a good guy and Brody is chill."

"They seem nice." I keep the part about Brody's future sister-in-law being my sister's best friend to myself. Being known as Essie's sister was something to be left back in high school.

My palms are sweaty by the time we reach the lobby. Chase links our fingers as we enter the hotel restaurant, where groups of students are gathered. Some have laptops, others are playing cards or talking.

"Chase! My man, you finally came out of hiding!" A guy at a table full of huge guys and pretty girls wearing makeup stands up and waves us over. His gaze snags on our clasped hands and his eyebrows rise.

Chase drops my hand and goes in for a fist bump and a back slap. I get curious looks from the guys. A couple of girls who actively ignore me in the dorm hallway or the bathroom whisper to each other. I suddenly feel like I'm under a microscope because there's too much attention on me. I shouldn't have let Chase entice me out of the room with promises of more oral-gasms.

He slings his arm over my shoulder. "Cammie, these are my friends, please don't hold it against me. Guys, this is Cammie, please don't talk shit about me to her."

I wave and am subsequently introduced to every person at the table. Of all the people there, only Brody has said hi to me before in passing. But I don't really give off an approachable vibe, either.

Chase grabs two chairs and crams us between his friend Gage and some girl who looks pretty unhappy to no longer be sitting beside Chase's buddy. The girls who ignore me in the bathroom are seated across from us. I've already forgotten their names thanks to nerves.

"So what floor do you live on?" the girl with long dark hair asks.

"Third."

The blonde girl tips her head. "Really? How come I've never seen you before?"

I shrug. This is literally the worst. I see them almost every day in the hall or the bathroom.

"I've never seen you with Chase before. How do you two know each other?" The dark-haired girl props her chin on her fist and smiles, like I'm suddenly the most interesting person in the world. But she gives me a visual sweep that tells me without words that she doesn't approve of this pairing.

Chase slings an arm over the back of my chair. "We ended up as roommates last night."

The dark-haired girl's eyes flare and she exchanges a knowing glance with her friend. "Right, that makes sense now."

"Was there only one bed?" the blonde girl asks with a smirk.

"And a pullout couch. But I broke that," Chase says helpfully, oblivious to the way he's basically setting me up to be his one-night stand.

"Yeah, you did." His teammate high-fives him.

I feel like the butt of a terrible joke, even as Chase tries to explain how it happened.

"What program are you in?" the blonde girl asks.

"Kinesiology, right?" Brody, who's sitting next to the dark-haired girl, asks.

"Uh yeah, but I'm double majoring in English."

"Double major? But like, doesn't that mean all you do is study?" the dark-haired girl asks.

I shrug. "I like books more than I like people." Now is one of those times when blunt honesty does not work to my advantage.

They snicker and turn their attention back to each other.

"How's Essie? She happy to be back in Toronto?" Brody asks.

Both the girls stop talking to focus on us.

"Who's Essie?" Chase asks, suddenly interested. Maybe I should have mentioned that Brody and I grew up in the same town.

"My older sister," I explain. "She misses things about Vancouver, but she missed being away from her bestie more. And it's definitely easier for her to be here, especially with the wedding and all."

"What wedding?" the girl beside Brody asks.

Brody doesn't so much as look their way when he answers. "My brother's." He drums on the table, maybe a little agitated since so many people are now focused on us. I relate. "Especially since Ess is Rix's maid of honor."

"Yeah. It made sense."

"Do you two know each other?" Chase asks, glancing between us.

Before I can answer, I'm cut off.

"Wait, isn't Tristan marrying Flip Madden's sister? Do you know the Maddens?" One of the girls beside Brody is suddenly super interested in me.

Which is one of the reasons I never mention the several-people-removed connection.

"My sister is friends with his sister," I explain.

"Did you ever go over to the Maddens' though? Or did Flip come to your house?" they press. "He's superhot. And apparently a freak in the sheets."

I've heard all about Flip Madden's reputation. And Tristan's, but who knows what's true and what's fiction.

"Phillip is like eight years older than Cammie; he would have been her babysitter if anything," Brody says with a roll of his eyes.

"Oh, right." The girls go back to ignoring me, and Brody changes the subject.

Someone else jumps in, allowing me to sink into my embarrassment.

Chase and his friends laugh and joke, and I sit there feeling less and less like I belong. And like Essie's popularity is still something I can't get out from under. I don't fit in with these people. His friends seem nice enough, but it's clear the girls don't want me here and when we're back in the dorms, they'll go right back to looking through me like they always have. Chase keeps his arm around me, but I don't know any of the people they're talking about, and he doesn't explain who they are so I can be in on the jokes.

After half an hour of listening to conversations happen around me, I decide I've had enough of being social. These people probably believe I'm just Chase's current hookup. There's a good chance I am. I know at least three girls who have made out with him in our dorm alone.

I push my chair back and Chase retracts his arm, still engaged in conversation with his teammates. It isn't until I stand that his attention shifts my way. His gaze moves over me on an appreciative sweep. "Where you going?"

My heart thunders in my chest as I thumb over my shoulder. "I have a couple assignments I need to tackle."

He frowns. "Want me to come back up with you?"

I wave a hand around. "Nah, it's cool. I need the quiet. You stay here and hang with your friends."

He tips his head, like he's trying to decide if he believes me. "I'll give you a little time then?"

I give him two thumbs-up. *Cool, Cammie, cool—not weird at all.*

The girls across from me smirk and whisper to each other.

Brody crosses his arms and side-eyes them.

I head back to the room where the only person I need to fit in with is myself.

CHAPTER 11

CHASE

Cammie's shoulders roll in as she heads for the elevator. She also pulls her hood up.

"Uh, I'm going to head up to the room, too."

Brody raises an eyebrow at me.

"Have fun with your new friend!" Barbie, who actually looks like an original Barbie, calls after me as I rush to catch up with Cammie.

I manage to reach the elevator in time, but unfortunately there are other people in there, so we just stand awkwardly beside each other until we get to the fourth floor. I follow Cammie down the hall and back into our room.

Cammie heads for her laptop.

"Things got weird." I cross my arms, then drop them at my sides. "And I don't know why."

Cammie sighs and tips her head up, eyes on the ceiling.

"What happened down there?"

She drops into the desk chair and spins to face me, tucking her hands into her pockets.

"I have schoolwork, and it wasn't like I was part of the conversations when you were walking down post-party lane. I don't know any of the people you were talking about. I don't get invited to parties, Chase, and usually I'm fine with that. I'm used to not fitting in, but shining a light on that doesn't seem like it'll be a lot of fun for me or you."

"You can come to a party with me, then you'll know more people." I realize I've never done this before. Tried to make someone I like feel included, and based on how unhappy Cammie looks, I'm not all that great at it. But I could get better.

"Is that really what you want? Because honestly, the way that rolled out down there made me sound like your hookup." She tugs on the string of her hoodie. "Which, I mean, I kind of am considering what's gone down in this room."

"That's not...I didn't mean...you're not—" I think back to the way I introduced her.

She shrugs. "It's okay, Chase. I'm not throwing shade, but you're already kind of a legend. And if I looked like you, I'd probably hook up all over the place, too."

I rub the back of my neck. "I haven't hooked up with that many girls."

She gives me a look.

"I mean..." For the past two months, most weekends have included a party. I'd meet some girl, we'd have some fun, and at the end of the night, I'd go home with my friends and the girl went home with her friends and that's that. Maybe I see a former hookup on campus and wave and say hi and then make an excuse about having class or practice. Shit. I'm kind of a douchebag.

"You don't get that good at giving orgasms by practicing on a pocket pussy." Cammie sighs. "I like you, Chase, but I'm kind of a fucking weirdo who would rather rewatch *Return of the King* a hundred times than play beer pong in my underwear."

"I like your weird, though." I leave the beer pong comment alone because I've done that mostly naked. I was in board shorts, though.

She smiles, but it looks sad, and I don't like it.

Both our phones chime.

Cammie pulls hers out of her hoodie. "Looks like we can go back to the dorms."

"Now?" I ask.

She nods and gives me a small smile. "Guess we should pack up." She stands and turns away as she crosses the room and grabs her backpack, tucking her laptop and other random items into it.

"But what about the deal we made? I owe you another orgasm." I know this is the wrong thing to offer, but I'm unsure how to fix this. I thought I had more time with her. What if this hotel room is all we'll ever have?

Before I drop to my knees and do something worse, like beg Cammie for the opportunity to bury my fingers and my face in her pussy before we leave, there's a knock on our door. "It's Colby, your resident advisor."

Cammie skirts around me and throws the door open, already wearing her backpack.

"Lovett and Lovelock, you've been released back to the dor—" His eyes flare as he takes in Cammie standing before him and me, still standing by the rumpled bed, the broken pullout couch behind me. There is no way I can broaden my stance wide enough to hide it. "What the fudge is going on in here? Where's your roommate, Lovett?"

"I'm standing right here." Cammie points to herself. "I'm Cameron Lovelock. Cammie for short." She points to me. "And that's Chase Lovett, which you and the rest of the campus already know."

"But, but." The color drains from Colby's face as he glances between us. "Why didn't either of you report the error? I would have reassigned one of you."

I tuck my hand into my pocket. "I did try to tell you, but you were dealing with a crier and told me it would have to wait until morning. We handled the situation on our own."

"But the couch is broken. How did the couch get broken?"

"Chase dove onto it once we set it up and it didn't survive

him," Cammie explains flatly as a flush works its way up her neck and into her cheeks.

"You only had one bed," Colby states.

"Yes," Cammie and I say at the same time.

"Chase, I need to speak to you in the hall." Colby tries to sound authoritative but his voice is all pitchy.

"I'm heading out so you two can have whatever discussion you need to have inside the room. I'll report the broken couch to the front desk."

"It's my fault it's broken, I can do it," I offer.

"It's fine. I really don't mind." Cammie turns to Colby. "Chase was a perfect gentleman last night. He offered to take the pullout couch and to sleep on the floor, so whatever lecture you're about to give him is probably unnecessary. Unless it's about the broken couch, but honestly, that thing is a piece of shit, and it was only a matter of time before someone fell through it. At least it was a virile, strapping young man and not some poor old guy who would have been stuck all night in the hole. Also, I have a black belt in karate and I can literally flip Chase over my shoulder." She salutes both of us. "See you back on campus."

Cammie slips past Colby and speed walks down the hall, disappearing down the stairs. At least this isn't like one of my party hookups and I can find her again without any trouble.

"There's no way she could flip you over her shoulder," Colby muses.

"She's not lying. She did it last night."

"I thought she said you were a perfect gentleman."

"I was. She was disoriented in the middle of the night when she used the bathroom and I scared her when she came out."

"Wow." Colby rubs the patchy scruff on his chin. "Can you do me a favor?"

"You don't want me to say anything about the mix-up with me ending up in a room with a pint-sized female-identifying student," I supply.

"I could get in a lot of shit."

"People already know."

"What people?"

"Brody and Gage."

"Shit."

"And maybe a few other people."

"Like who? You better not spread rumors about her."

I tuck a hand into my pocket and frown. "I wouldn't do that."

"You better mean that. Pack up and head back to campus." Colby leaves me standing in the middle of the room, wishing we'd been stuck here longer than one night.

CHAPTER 12

CAMMIE

I return to my dorm. The whole building smells like campfire and dirty wet socks. I disappear to the library and hole myself up there so I can work on my freaking creative writing submission. Unsurprisingly, I get distracted and work on my fanfic instead, finishing up the chapter with the double sixty-niner.

In my story, Arwen sits on Aragorn's (Chase's) face while sucking them both off. Then Legolas eats Arwen's pussy while Aragorn eats her ass before the three of them have filthy sex. Within an hour, I have more than a hundred reviews and readers are begging for more.

@THEREALOPHELIA

That update was hot! How was your night with the hockey player? Is that chapter drawing from real life experience?

@LEGAGORNSANDWICH

It was fun but now we're back in the dorms.

@THEREALOPHELIA

OMGGGGGGGG. Come on! I need more details than that. I can't wait until I'm in university next year.

@LEGAGORNSANDWICH

I suggest an off-campus apartment. The whole dorm smells like three-day-old wet socks.

@THEREALOPHELIA

Ew. That sounds awful. But seriously, what happened last night?

I debate how much I want to say over messages. I honestly hope Chase isn't out there telling his friends about getting a blow job from the residence freak. How humiliating would that be? But O is my best friend. Sure, we've never met in real life, but we talk every day. And she's applying to programs here next year.

@LEGAGORNSANDWICH

We made out and got each other off. It was *chef's kiss*

I bite my lip after I press send and wait for her reply. I'm not disappointed. A slew of GIFs ranging from shock to fainting to cheerleaders dancing follows.

@THEREALOPHELIA

OMG! You made out with the hockey player! Are you going to hang out again?

I think about how awkward it was with his friends. He has his own life, and I have mine. Last night was fun, and sure I'd love to do it again, but it's probably better for both of us (namely me) if I treat it like a fever dream. Then I'm less likely to get hurt when I see some other girl hanging off his arm.

@LEGAGORNSANDWICH

I don't know. It was fun, but probably just a one-time thing.

I don't love the way that makes my stomach flip in a not-good way.

I spend another hour in the library, working on my creative writing submission for once, and finishing up an assignment for my English class before I return to the dorms. I take the long way to my room to avoid the common area and manage to slip inside my room without running into anyone.

I swear there's a knock on my door around eleven, just as I'm falling asleep, but then I hear Colby in the hall, telling someone it's past curfew and people are trying to sleep.

The next morning I'm up and out early. I spend the hours between classes at the library again instead of in my room. It's helpful for completing assignments. And I make a little more headway on my submission. I also start another chapter of my story, with the three of them traveling to meet with a dwarf contact. They're gathering information as they work with Sam to save the Shire from Saruman, but now, they've stopped for the night. Writing the smutty stuff in a public place feels weird, though, so I save it for later tonight, when I'm alone in my room.

My nerves are at an all-time high as I make my way to biology later that afternoon. All I could manage for lunch was a blueberry muffin. I pull my hood up and slide into a seat in the middle of the lecture theater. I focus on setting up my tablet so I can take notes and avoid searching for the one person I've been hiding from but desperately want to see.

A body drops into the seat next to me. I'm hit with a waft of familiar cologne. My nether region drools, my nipples tighten, and a kaleidoscope of butterflies unleashes in my stomach. Chase is sitting beside me. In class.

"Hey." That single word feels like a caress on bare skin.

I glance at him, mouth going dry as my heart skips a beat and then takes off at a gallop. "Hey."

His gaze moves over my face, and he swallows thickly before he asks, "Is it cool if I sit here?"

"If you want," I croak.

"I haven't seen you around since we got back into the dorms." It's mostly an observation, with a hint of accusation.

"I've been at the library working on assignments," I offer weakly.

He arches a brow. "And avoiding me?"

"I didn't want to make it awkward." Guess I failed at that.

"I knocked on your door three times yesterday. And left a note on your message board," Chase says.

"You did?" I was probably so focused on getting into my room without running into anyone, that I didn't even look at the whiteboard stuck to my door.

"The message is still there. Didn't you sleep in your room last night?" His jaw tics.

"What's this?" I poke his cheek.

"What's what?"

"There's a muscle jumping in your jaw."

His nostrils flare and he leans in closer, dropping his voice to a whisper and brushing his lips on the shell of my ear. "I like you. I missed you." I feel him take a deep breath before continuing. "And the idea of someone else touching your precious when I want it to be mine makes me unhappy."

I lean back so I can see his face. He looks serious. I can't believe we're having this conversation in the middle of a lecture theater that's quickly filling with students. "Why would you automatically assume if I didn't sleep in my bed I slept in someone else's and allowed them access to my body? I'm not the Hookup Champion between the two of us."

"I don't know. But I didn't see you at all yesterday and I didn't like it, and I also didn't get a chance to get your phone number and I've spent the last twenty-four hours in worst-case scenario-ville," he admits.

"Oh."

Brody drops into the seat next to him. His hood is pulled up to conceal his face. Looks like we're both hiding from the world, but probably for very different reasons.

"Hey, Cammie. Hey, Chase." He waves and starts pulling things out of his backpack.

"Hey," we say in unison.

Another large guy sits down who I presume must also be on the school hockey team based on his size and haircut—most of these guys sport a slightly shaggy mop covered with a Tilton University or Terror ball cap. Except for Brody. He usually sports a plain black one.

He greets Brody and Chase, then leans forward to give me a two-finger wave. "You must be Cammie."

Chase's head whips around in his direction. "Dude."

Brody stifles a snicker.

"What? This *is* the girl you were talking about at the gym earlier, right? The edgy one you can fit in your pocket?"

Chase called me edgy? And that he could fit me in his pocket? Both are true, I guess. My wardrobe is fairly monochromatic and next to him I'm pretty darn small. But what else did he say about me?

"I'm Mac. I play defense for the Blaze. Chase couldn't stop talking about you through our entire workout. I get it, you're cute." He winks.

"I will end you if you keep it up," Chase growls.

My entire body likes that sound.

I lean into Chase and extend my hand. It means my boob is pressed against his forearm and my cheek brushes his chest. Brody leans back, smirk firmly in place as Mac's grin widens. He takes my small hand in his giant mitt and gives it a light shake. "I'm Cammie, the pocket-sized edgy girl Chase apparently couldn't stop talking about. It's nice to meet you."

"It's nice to meet *you*, Cammie." Mac is ridiculously flirty. Everything about him screams one-night stand.

"Don't use that tone with Cammie," Chase grumbles.

Mac gives him a two-finger salute. "Sir, yes, sir." He winks at me again and leans back in his seat.

The professor takes her place at the front of the lecture hall, ending any further conversation. It's hard to focus on her with Chase sitting beside me. He rests his knee against mine and leans into my space to look at my notes every few minutes. He smells divine and it takes literally every ounce of resolve not to reach out and trace the thick veins on the back of his hand.

After class, Mac throws out a blanket invitation to go to the campus pub.

"Who will be there?" Brody asks.

"A few of the guys from the team." He adjusts his ball cap. "And probably those girls from your dorm, Barbie and what's her name?"

"Annabelle," Brody supplies.

"Yeah. That's right."

"I've got a chemistry assignment I need to tackle, but thanks," Brody says. "I'm going to hit the library so I can grab a couple of research books, but I'll catch you all later."

Mac turns to Chase. "You're going to bail too, aren't you? Don't make me ask Gage to come with me."

"Oh yeah. Definitely bailing. Have fun."

"You suck." He fires the bird at Chase, then turns his megawatt smile on me. "You want to ditch him and come with me?"

"It's a tempting offer, but I'm good, thanks," I deadpan and hug Chase's well-developed biceps.

"That was a test, and you passed. I like this one." He claps Chase on the back and ambles off. He doesn't make it ten feet before he's accosted by a group of girls.

"He's…interesting."

"He flirts with literally everyone."

"Yeah. I gathered that."

"I've never seen him hook up with someone though."

"Wait, seriously? Not even kiss anyone?" It's hard to believe, but I guess you can't always judge a book by its cover, or its flirtiness.

"Nope. Not even a peck." Chase looks at me. "You heading back to res?"

"Yeah. I have a night class but I'm stopping by my room first. How about you?"

He nods, gaze moving over my face as he tucks his finger under my backpack strap. "I can carry this for you."

"I have a black belt; I can handle a backpack."

"I know. But I'd like to carry your books for you, all nineteen-fifties-style chivalrous like."

I tip my head. "Is this to make up for the unchivalrous face fuck on the hotel bed?"

His eyes flare.

"Which I loved, by the way," I tack on, in case he thinks otherwise. I'm pretty sure all my moaning and humming and generally pleased noises should have tipped him off to that fact already.

"Yes. No. Yes. I loved that too, so fucking much. But we shouldn't talk about it right now or I'll need to use your back-pack or maybe even your body as a shield because it's making things happen in my pants." Chase half-groans that statement as his eyes heat.

I lick my lips and glance down at his crotch.

"Don't do that; he'll know you're looking and embarrass me," he whispers.

"We don't want that." I hand him my backpack and he falls into step beside me as we make the trek across campus to our residence building. "So you were talking about me to your hockey bros," I say conversationally. I can't believe he's walking me back to res. And carrying my books for me. I feel like I'm in a movie right now.

"I thought you were avoiding me. Which you were, and I wasn't sure what I'd done wrong or if I could fix it," he admits. "So I told the guys about you, and Brody mentioned that Barbie and Annabelle, while sometimes helpful in keeping the hard-core fans at bay, can also be super bitches to basically everyone who isn't a hockey player."

"They don't exactly exude warmth."

"They really don't. He also mentioned that not everyone is a high-level extrovert like myself, and that sometimes it's important to check in on my quiet friends to make sure they're not swimming in a mental lake of terror when they're put in situations that are outside of their comfort zone," Chase adds.

"That's an astute observation." Brody seems nice.

"Brody is an astute guy," Chase agrees as he adjusts my backpack straps.

It's not light. I have three textbooks in there and each one must weigh eight pounds. But he's a hockey player so he can handle it, I'm sure.

Some guy comes up to Chase to ask him about an upcoming game, and we end up stuck chatting for a couple minutes. Chase keeps looking at me as he talks about the other team. It feels uncomfortable just standing here, while he's told how well everyone needs to play or risk disappointing the entire campus.

"Is it like that for all of you?" I ask. "You had to be the best of the best in your high school to play here. Is it overwhelming to have everyone put their expectations on you like that?"

"It comes with the territory. We're all used to being the best. Now most of us are at the same level, with a few standouts."

"Are you one of the standouts?" I ask out of genuine curiosity.

"I want to be. Brody definitely is. Even as a first year, the potential is there. He has so much natural talent. I think he'll be even better than his brother at some point, as long as he doesn't get too in his head about it."

I nod slowly, absorbing that information. "Do you get in your head about it?"

Chase shrugs. "I think we all do at some point. University is tough. Between classes, practice, workouts, homework, and a social life, it's hard not to get swept up in all the fun stuff and forget that this is step one of a much bigger goal."

"To finish a degree and make the pros?" I ask, fascinated.

"Basically, yeah."

"You're an interesting guy, Chase."

"You think so?" The smile that lights up his face makes my heart flutter.

"Definitely." I've never been friends with an athlete before. It's a lot of responsibility and dedication. They have to function as part of a team and juggle all the same things I do on top of that.

He opens the door to our residence building. Half a dozen people say hi to him while we wait for the elevator. People ask if he's coming out tonight and he deflects saying he has assignments and early practice. We cram ourselves into the elevator and Chase pulls me into a corner and moves me to stand in front of him, settling a hand on my waist while we ascend.

More people say hi to him and give me curious looks as we walk down the hall to my room.

The note I didn't notice from yesterday is still on my whiteboard.

Can I please have your number?
CL

I tip my head up and smile, feeling shy. "Yes, you can have my number."

"Cool." He pulls out his phone, snaps a quick picture, adds my name, and passes me the device.

I key in my number and hand it back. My phone pings a second later.

I pull it out and show him the text he just sent me. "Got yours now, too." It's only five thirty. I don't have to leave for class for another hour. "Do you want to come in for a bit?"

"Yeah." Chase nods, then shakes his head. "But no."

I try not to let the disappointment show on my face, but I'm pretty sure I fail.

"If I come into your room, I'm going to want to do things."

"Kinda the point." I wish I had my backpack to hold on to so I don't fidget.

Chase smiles. "I want to show you I like you more than just a hookup."

He looks so determined, and I like it. "Okay."

"So maybe tomorrow morning I can meet you for coffee after my practice?"

"Sure. Yeah. I'd like that." I think he just asked me on a coffee date.

"Cool. Awesome. That's great. I'll text you later."

"Okay."

He bites his lip and his eyes dart to mine.

"Can I kiss you, though?"

"Yes, please."

He drops both of our backpacks and nods at someone as they pass. He glances over his shoulder, waiting until they disappear around the corner before his warm palm curves around the side of my neck. I tip my head up as he drops his.

He brushes his lips over mine, then pulls the bottom one between his, sucking softly. We make matching needy sounds as our bodies gravitate closer. We angle our heads at the same time. Our tongues meet and brush against each other. I settle a hand on his biceps and give it a happy little squeeze.

"Lovett, Lovelock, if you do that on the other side of the door, no one has to witness it," Colby shouts from not very far away.

I free my lips from Chase's and pull my hood up. Chase's lips press into a line and he gives Colby the death stare.

"I'm helping you out here, man. Your buddy Gage just snapped a picture. You're welcome. If you need condoms, you can visit the health center." He saunters past us, wearing a satisfied grin.

Chase thumbs over his shoulder. "I'm going to go beat up Gage."

"Good luck."

"Thanks." He kisses my cheek and grabs his bag, rushing down the hall as he shouts, "Steele, I'm coming for you!"

I can't stop smiling. I have so much to tell Tally.

CHAPTER 13

CHASE

"So what's the deal with you and your hotel roomie?" Gage asks as we're changing back into street clothes after practice.

"Her name is Cammie," I correct.

"What's the deal with you and *Cammie*?" He stresses her name.

"I like her."

"I figured that with the way you were sucking face in the hall. You sure it's a good idea to hook up with one of the girls on our floor? Sort of limits your options unless you're aiming for awkwardness when you move on to the next one." He pulls a shirt over his head, covering the tattoo on his chest.

"I'm not planning to move on to the next one." I spray deodorant under my arms, then give it an extra courtesy spritz for good measure.

Gage stops messing with his hair to gape at me. "Dude."

"What?"

"We're two months into four years of fun times."

Brody rolls his eyes.

Gage points an accusing finger at him. "Don't even. Your

monk status is ninety percent of the reason girls won't leave you alone. Mac at least flirts with them."

"I don't want to spend the next four years racking up a ridiculous number of one-night stands," I say, and mean it. I thought a lot about what Cammie said about my reputation and it just isn't what I want for myself.

"This," Brody agrees.

"But I need a wingman at parties!" Gage argues. "Someone other than Mac because all the girls want him more. Please. I beg of you."

"You'll be fine without a wingman," I assure him. "Honestly, the last couple of months were fun, but it gets old fast."

Running into former hookups sucks. It's awkward and uncomfortable and I started to feel used. I want more than someone to get off with. I want to watch movies and study and hang out with Cammie while she writes a new chapter as much as I want to feel her lips on mine. I want her to be my person, and I want to be hers.

"You guys suck." Gage stuffs his hair supplies in his backpack. "I gotta roll. I have tutoring in fifteen." He flips us both the bird and takes off.

Brody and I finish getting dressed and leave the locker room. I check my phone as we step outside. "I'm meeting up with Cammie for coffee and walking her to class," I tell him.

"Good," Brody replies. "Have you asked her on a date yet?"

"Isn't coffee a date?"

"I mean, I guess. But you've sort of jumped over the whole coffee-get-to-know-you phase since you've already spent the night together."

"So you think I should take her on a *date* date?" I run a hand through my hair.

He side-eyes me. "Yeah, you definitely should."

"I haven't been on a date since the beginning of senior year," I admit.

"I know this. And taking a girl to Mickey D's doesn't count as a real date."

"It felt like a date. I paid," I say defensively.

"For fries and a milkshake."

"It seemed legit at the time," I grumble.

He exhales his annoyance through his nose dramatically. "Take her out for dinner and go to a movie or something. Spend some time with just her. And don't be in a rush to get her back into a bed."

I blow out a breath. "What if *she* wants to get back into a bed with me?"

"You haven't had sex yet, right?" I didn't give Brody details, but he knows things happened.

I shake my head. "We just did other stuff."

He nods his approval. "Do more other stuff. And always take care of her first. My brother may not have been the best role model when it came to how he handled relationships until he and Rix became a thing, but that was the rule he stressed. Always take care of her before you get yours. Give before you get. He also says it's important to listen first and react second."

"It's solid advice."

"And make sure you take her somewhere the team doesn't go. You don't want to run into a former hookup when you're on a date with Cammie," Brody advises.

"Good call."

We arrive at the coffee shop and Brody continues to his next class. I wait outside until Cammie arrives. She's wearing a black *Lord of the Rings* hoodie and a pair of wide-leg jeans. She looks fucking adorable.

A beautiful smile lights up her face as she approaches. "Hey."

"Hey, yourself." When she's close enough, I tug on the loose end of a backpack strap and pull her into me.

She tips her head up and I bend, but she leans away. "What are you doing?"

"Saying hi."

"People are going to think we're a thing."

"Good. I want us to be a thing." I stroke her cheek with a single finger. "Can I please kiss you?"

"Right now?" She glances around.

"Yeah. Right now." She's so cute. I can't remember the last time a girl didn't want to kiss me in front of everyone. It's refreshing to be wanted for more than my athlete status.

"Okay?"

"You don't sound very sure about that."

Her tongue darts out. "You can kiss me."

I dip down and brush my lips over hers. Little electric bursts of pleasure zing through my veins. I slide my fingers into her hair and tilt my head, my tongue stroking along the seam of her lips. They part on a soft gasp and she grips my shirt, tipping her head, letting me in. I sink into the kiss, into the feel of her lips on mine, relishing the softness and the sweet aftertaste of strawberry on her tongue.

"Get a room, Lovett!" one of my asshole teammates shouts as he passes by.

Cammie pushes on my chest and steps back, quickly pulling her hood up to hide her face.

I flip off my teammate, then wrap an arm around her shoulder and guide her into the coffee shop. I'm hit with the scent of slightly burnt cheese and coffee. And I'm suddenly starving. Which is a common occurrence.

We get in line and Cammie fidgets nervously.

"You okay?"

"Yeah. Great. Awesome. Good."

"You sure?"

"Absolutely." She gives me two thumbs-up.

A couple of girls and a guy stop to say hi. One of them wishes me good luck at the game tonight.

"How was your first class this morning?" I ask.

"Good. It was good. Except for the pop quiz. That wasn't

awesome, but I think I did okay. How about yours? Oh wait, you had practice, not class. How was practice?"

"It was also good. One of the guys put a poster of Scarlet Reed in Gage's locker and his face turned bright red before I watched him secretly fold it up to save for later."

Two more people interrupt to say hi. And then two more.

"Everyone knows you," Cammie whispers.

I shrug.

We reach the counter, and I order half the food from the display case and a quarter sweet latte and turn to Cammie. "What would you like?"

She seems surprised by the offer. "Oh, I can get my own."

I tip my head and arch a brow. "I would like to get your coffee this morning, please, Cammie."

"I would like a caramel choco-latte with extra whipped cream," she says, somewhat grudgingly.

"Anything to eat?" I press.

"No thanks. I'm good."

I hand over my debit card and pay for the order, then stand off to the side and wait for everything to be ready. More people come up and talk to me, including a girl who was hanging out with us at the hotel. Cammie pulls her hood up and digs her phone out of her pocket.

I don't want to mess this up. My palms start to sweat. I don't know the girl's name, but I introduce Cammie. It works. She tells us her name is Hayley and we chat for a few minutes about classes and our upcoming game against Kingston U.

Finally, they call my name and I grab the armload of snacks and my drink, and Cammie takes hers. She dips her finger into the whipped cream, piled so high she can't put a lid on it yet, and makes eye contact with me as she sucks it clean.

The image of her lips wrapped around my cock, her face cupped in my hands while I fucked her mouth, slams into my brain like a freight train.

My hard-on is instantaneous. I barely manage to contain my groan. I give her a look.

She arches a brow. "What?"

I lean down until my mouth is at her ear. "I know how talented that pretty mouth is."

I straighten and her smile grows devious.

Taking Brody's advice might not be the worst idea. Especially if other stuff includes Cammie's sweet, gorgeous mouth.

I follow her out of the coffee shop, thankful my hoodie covers the growing problem behind my fly. She dips her finger in the whipped cream and sucks her finger clean again.

"Now you're just torturing me," I grumble.

"Yup."

"How's the writing? Did you finish another chapter? I want to know if the king of the dwarves knows how to help them."

"I'm working on one now," she replies.

"When can I read it?"

"When it's finished. But I can send you a little snippet later." We stop in front of the English building. "This is me. Thanks for the coffee."

"Thanks for the torment." Now's my chance. I can ask her to hang out. But I have a scrimmage tonight. It's the perfect opportunity. "So I have hockey tonight—"

"You'll be great." She nods and sips her drink.

"Maybe you want to come watch me play?" I've read her fanfic, which she loves to write. It would be cool if she came to see me do what I love, too.

She shuffles from foot to foot. "Oh. Um. I have this big assignment I'm working on."

"Right. Homework is important." I try to be cool even though it feels like rejection. I want her to like me as much as I like her.

"But another time might work," she tacks on. "And you can always knock on my door when you get back tonight. If it's not too late."

"For sure." My bag is full of snacks, but my appetite has disappeared.

"I should get to class." She thumbs over her shoulder, bites her lip, then closes the distance between us, pushes up on her tiptoes, and presses her lips to the edge of my jaw. "Thanks again for the coffee." She waves and nearly slams into someone when she turns around.

She pulls her hood up and rushes up the steps.

She kissed me. And invited me to knock on her door later tonight. It's progress. And I'll take it.

CHAPTER 14

CAMMIE

"Did I see you with Chase Lovett?" Tally whispers as she moves her backpack from the seat next to her. Her long blonde hair is pulled back in a ponytail. Her eyes are rimmed with black liner that makes her blue eyes pop, and her lips are glossy and pink. She's super pretty but a little edgy, which I appreciate.

I make a cringey face as I sink down in my seat, glancing around to make sure no one is paying attention to us. "Maybe."

She raises a perfectly tweezed eyebrow, keeping her voice low. "He's kind of hot shit around here."

"I know. I'll fill you in after class."

The professor steps up to the podium and begins the lecture on the themes in the book we're currently reading. I scribble notes on my tablet, trying to stay engaged, but my mind is on Chase and whatever is going on with him.

At the end of class, I pack up and Tally and I leave the building together. The hailstorm-tornado has long passed, and while it's cold, it's not the bone-chilling blustery kind that's coming for us in December. "Okay, I need the details on this whole Chase Lovett-walking-you-to-class business."

I fill her in on the residence building fiasco and the sprinklers going off.

"Oh my God, that's the worst. You could have messaged. I would have given you my room and stayed at my boyfriend's," she says.

"It was one in the morning, and it all happened kind of fast. Plus, we were in the middle of a storm and the hotel was down the street as opposed to across campus," I explain. Tally lives in apartment-style residences. They have their own kitchen and living room. We've only been sitting beside each other for a couple of weeks. We've gone for coffee a few times and a study-lunch twice. Of my two friends, I think she's the one Essie would like the most.

"That's fair." She adjusts her backpack. "So how did that lead to you and Chase becoming a thing?"

I explain the rest of the story, but gloss over the details for reasons.

"Holy shit. That is like…wow."

"I know. Like what is even happening? How did I manage to catch Chase's attention, right?"

Tally's brows pull together. "You're like, super cool, and freaking beautiful."

I laugh. "I'm weird. Trust me, my sister is the cool, pretty one. I'm more like the gremlin that only ventures out of the cave for ramen or hot elves."

"Oh my God, stop." Tally laughs. "Imagining you as a gremlin will give me nightmares. And everyone is weird. I like salty black licorice, and I've watched the movie *Step Up* probably two hundred times. I know every single dance routine by heart."

"Okay, I'll give you the salty black licorice. But I've probably watched the *LotR* trilogy just as many times."

"Point made then; everyone is a little weird." Her lips pull to the side. "So what's the deal with you and Chase? Are you a thing?"

"Um…I don't know?"

"He walked you to class, though?"

"Yeah. And yesterday he sat beside me in our bio class, and then walked me back to the dorms, asked me for my number, and kissed me good night. And then today he bought me a coffee, and he asked me to come to his game tonight." It does sound a lot like maybe we're seeing each other.

"Guys don't normally do all those things if they're not super interested," Tally says helpfully.

I tug on the string of my hoodie. "I said I had an assignment tonight and couldn't come to his game. Was that the wrong thing to do?"

"Do you actually have an assignment, or were you making an excuse?"

"Uhhhhh…I mean I always have an assignment to work on."

She arches a brow.

"It's not that I don't want to see him play. I do. I mean, it's probably pretty fun to watch a live game." Essie's gone to a few with Rix and says it's a blast.

Tally purses her lips, does a little hip-shimmy thing, and twitches her nose. "I'm going to tell you something."

She exhales what seems like a slightly stressed breath. Mostly when we hang out we talk about assignments and what it's like to live on campus.

My spine straightens. "Okay." I hope it's not something bad about Chase.

"My dad is the head coach for the Terror." She whispers it like she's expecting a death knell to follow.

"Like for the pro hockey team?" I whisper back.

"Yeah." She swallows thickly. This revelation seems to make her super uncomfortable.

"My sister's best friend is engaged to Tristan Stiles?" I don't know why that comes out like a question.

Tally's eyebrows shoot up. "Do you mean Rix Madden?"

"Yeah." This is so fucking weird.

"Wait, Essie is your sister?" Tally asks.

"You know Essie?" What the fuck is happening?

"Yeah. She's like an honorary member of the Badass Babe Brigade," Tally replies.

"Of course she is," I mutter. "I don't even know what the Badass Babe Brigade is but that tracks with Essie." And it sounds cool. Like something I wish I was part of.

"It's our girl group. This is so wild. Like what are the actual chances? Rix goes to school here, too." She's all excited now.

"Ess mentioned that she was taking classes again, but I figured she's off campus, right?" Me not wanting Essie to connect me with her friends ends up with me being friends with her friends anyway. Not to mention Brody living on my floor makes me feel like I should just accept being forever known as Essie's little sister.

"For the most part, but we have lunch once a week." Her eyes light up and she bounces on the balls of her feet. "You should come next time!"

"Oh, I wouldn't want to intrude." I haven't seen Rix in a long time—like since I was fourteen. She was always nice to me, but I was a hard-core hobbiter even back then.

"You wouldn't be! She'd be so happy to see you!" Tally seems very big on being inclusive. "Anyway, back to Chase inviting you to his game and you saying you have an assignment. Why don't you want to go?"

"We always seem to run into one of his former hookups. I end up just standing there awkwardly like I don't belong. Then to make it less fun, there are these girls who are always hanging around them who are sort of..." I try to find a word to describe them that isn't steeped in negativity. It's not easy.

"Bitches?" Tally supplies.

"They're not super warm."

Tally rolls her eyes. "They're puck bunnies. They chase after the players. Some puck bunnies are legit super nice, but other ones—it's like a game to them to bag a player. Ignore them."

"I'd like to, but two of them live on my floor." And I'm a

thousand percent sure they go to all the games. "And I don't know a ton about hockey." Other than the little I've caught in the common room while making ramen.

"I can give you a crash course. I can't go to tonight's game, but I can probably go to the next one with you," Tally offers.

"Do you actually want to go to a university hockey game? Does it pale in comparison to the pro games?" I have no idea. "Wouldn't it be annoying for you? Like won't people know who you are and be all like super friendly with you like they are with Brody?"

"He's a nice kid."

I want to mention that we're all the same age, but I feel like her life experiences and mine probably differ significantly. She's grown up around professional hockey players. What a weird life.

"Can't be easy with his brother being way more visible than my dad." Tally twirls a lock of hair around her finger, expression pensive. "And yeah, it's sort of the same. It's more like when the players find out who my dad is, suddenly they want to take me on dates."

I wrinkle my nose. "Ew."

"Having a boyfriend has helped with that, though." She shrugs. "Anyway, the offer stands. If you want company at a game, I'd be your wingwoman."

"Cool. Okay. I appreciate that."

"I have dance practice soon, so I have to go, but I'll message you later!"

I accept a hug and she flits off.

Essie would be so proud. It seems I've made myself a real friend, even if my sister was friends with her first.

And I'm seeing a guy. The hottest guy.

What a week.

CHAPTER 15

CAMMIE

I've just finished uploading my newest chapter when there's a knock at my door. It's ten thirty. I close my laptop and check my reflection in the mirror before I put my eye to the peephole.

Standing outside my room is Chase. Based on the state of his hair, he's fresh from the shower. He waves at someone as they pass, then runs his hand through his hair and stuffs it in his pocket.

My stomach fills with butterflies and my heart slams itself excitedly around in my chest. I do a breath-freshness check, deem myself Chase ready, and open the door. "Hey."

"Hi." The right side of his mouth quirks up in a shy smile.

"How was the game?"

"Good. We won. Did you finish your assignment?"

"It's about fifty percent finished." I make a face. I got distracted by my fanfic, as usual. "If you won, shouldn't you be out celebrating?"

"It was just a scrimmage, not an official game. Those are on the weekends. And I wanted to see you." He chews on the corner of his lip.

"Do you want to come in?" I step back.

"Is that okay? Or we can hang out in the common room if that's better for you?" He runs a hand through his hair. Then stuffs it in his pocket. Again.

Two guys pass him and he's forced to withdraw it almost immediately so he can fist-bump them. They both say hi to me, too. "The common room doesn't seem better for you." He's more likely to be inundated by people who want his attention. And I don't feel like sharing him right now.

He shrugs.

I hook my finger around his and tug.

He steps over the threshold, and I close the door behind him.

His gaze bounces around my room, then lands on the posters above my bed. "The pretty one's Arwen?"

"And the hot guys are Legolas and Aragorn." I stuff my hands in my hoodie.

"I can see the allure." Chase rubs his bottom lip.

"Of Arwen?" I ask.

"Of the three of them together." His gaze shifts back to me. "Did you finish the next chapter?"

"Maybe."

"Can I maybe read it?"

"If you want." I tap the back of my computer chair. I'm already getting sweaty, and the full body tingles have started just from the thought.

He drops into my chair and it groans under his weight. He has to lower the chair so his knees don't hit the desk. When I move to stand next to him, he spins the chair and pulls me into his lap, then moves to face the computer again.

"Fuck, I'm excited." He flips the laptop open.

The screen blinks to life. Arwen, Aragorn, and Legolas stare back at us. I use my fingerprint to unlock the computer, and the chapter appears on the website. I hit refresh and am thrilled to see there are already two hundred reviews.

"Legagorn Sandwich, very creative." Chase wraps his arm around my waist.

"What are you doing?"

"Cuddling with you while I read this." He moves my hair out of the way and kisses my neck. "Will you scroll for me?"

"Sure."

He rests his chin on my shoulder. Chase's hard chest presses against my back and his free hand settles high on my right thigh. His hands are so big. Again, his lips move as he reads and every so often, he kisses my neck and inhales deeply.

"Oh fuck." The hand on my thigh clenches. "Holy shit." He bites the edge of my jaw. "You wrote *the scene*."

I turn my head in his direction. "I did."

His hot gaze moves to my mouth and the arm around my waist loosens. He cups my cheek in his palm and pulls my mouth to his. It's awkward with me sitting in his lap, but I swear I feel his erection against my ass. I roll my hips. He groans into my mouth and deepens the kiss. I cover the hand on my thigh and move it between my legs. I'm wearing pajama pants, so the sensation is muted, but still.

He tears his mouth from mine. "Wait!"

I startle and hop out of his lap, then stumble and almost lose my footing because my legs are like overcooked noodles.

"Sorry. Fuck. Sorry. Shit." He pushes out of the computer chair. His gaze darts back to my laptop. I swear there's real longing in his eyes.

But then…then I notice the very excessive problem in Chase's pants. I lick my lips. I can't help it. It's a reflex.

"Oh my God. Please don't do that." Chase shoves his hands in his hair and grips it tightly.

"Don't do what?" I have no idea what is happening right now.

"Look at me like that. Lick your delightful fucking lips like that," he groans.

"Not all of you seems to mind."

He bends at the waist, like he's in pain. "Fuuuuuccck."

"Are you okay?"

"Yes. No. Fuck." He flings a hand toward my laptop. "I can't read that right now. I really want to. Fuck. But if I do, I'm going to want to do other things."

"We can do other things," I reassure him.

"No. We can't."

It's hard to swallow humiliation, but I manage.

He must read my mortification on my face because he raises a hand. "It's not that I don't want to. I do. So fucking badly. But I want to take you on a date first. I like you. I like touching you, and reading your smutty fanfic, and acting out scenes that you might want to write into future chapters, but I also just like *you*. So before I'm allowed to touch your precious again with any of my body parts, and before you touch my sword of lust again with your soft, pretty hands or your talented, delightful mouth…" He adjusts his hard-on with a deep groan. "Please allow me the honor of taking you out for dinner. And a movie. *The Hobbit* is playing at the vintage theater tomorrow night. If you're free."

"I'm free."

"Awesome. Great." He grips the back of my computer chair and rolls it so it forms a barricade between us. "I want to hang out with you, but I'm in a pretty heightened state." He thumbs over his shoulder. "So I'm going to go back to my room and hopefully Brody is out so I can deal with my situation."

"I could leave my room for a few minutes if you're concerned."

Chase's jaw flexes. "Don't offer me that. I'll probably fuck your pillow." He glances at my bed and swallows thickly. "I'll definitely fuck your pillow."

I pick up my glasses cleaning cloth and hold it out to him. "You can take this with you."

He plucks it from my fingers without making contact, fists it, and gives me an imploring look as he brings it to his nose and sniffs. "I'm never giving this back."

"I have like twenty."

"Cool. Knock on my door tomorrow at six?"

"I can do that."

"Awesome." He backs toward the door and fumbles for the knob. "I can't wait to eat you for dinner."

I doubt he realizes what he just said. "Me neither." I slowly walk towards him as he frantically tries to exit my room.

He gets the door open and steps into the hall. I grab the front of his shirt.

"Cammie," he groans.

I tug, forcing him to bend. Is this what sexy, powerful women feel like? I'm a human weapon, bringing this huge, hot man-boy to his knees. Proverbially speaking. He holds the door open just enough that his head fits through.

"I hope you're good and hungry tomorrow night, Chase, because my pussy is on the dessert menu." I suck his bottom lip, dragging it between my teeth before I release him.

He stumbles backward two steps. "For the love of God, Cammie, close the fucking door."

I do. And turn the lock. The knob rattles. Chase makes a desperate sound on the other side and pounds on it with his fist. I flip the lock again and open it two inches. He's on his knees in front of the door. "Don't forget, I have a black belt; I can take you down."

He grips the jambs. "The next twenty hours will be the most delicious torture."

"Sweet dreams, Chase." I wink and close the door again.

"What the fuck is wrong with you, Lovett?"

"Fuck you, Gage."

"Chase? Are you okay?" a female voice asks.

"Barbiebelle, I'm not in the mood." A few moments later a door closes heavily down the hall.

Fifteen minutes later my phone dings with a message.

CHASE

I'm going to need another one of those cloth things because I have to wash this one and then it won't smell like you anymore.

I hug my phone to my chest and grin at the ceiling where Legolas and Aragorn stare down at me.

"He's a little obsessed with me."

It's a heady feeling, having someone as amazing as Chase want me with such fervor. And I think I like it.

CHAPTER 16

CAMMIE

@THEREALOPHELIA

I'm so excited for your date night!

@LEGAGORNSANDWICH

Me toooooo! My sister is calling soon to walk me through wardrobe and makeup.

@THEREALOPHELIA

I need details when you get back! Or tomorrow!

@LEGAGORNSANDWICH

@THEREALOPHELIA

Oh and your last chapter was

@LEGAGORNSANDWICH

Thank you!

A message pops up from my sister with a one-minute warning.

@LEGAGORNSANDWICH

My sister's calling! Gotta go!

@THEREALOPHELIA

Have the best time!

@LEGAGORNSANDWICH

I will!

My phone rings a few seconds later.

"Hey! Hi! Hey!" I practically yell at my sister's two-dimensional form.

She arches a brow. "Take a breath."

I suck in air and motion to my face and what's under my neck. "I need your help. I have a date in an hour and I want to look good."

Essie shrieks. Loudly. "This is so exciting! What's his name? How did you meet him? What's his major?"

"His name is Chase. He's a kin major and we have some classes together." I avoid disclosing the whole hotel room situation, or the fact that we live in the same building, on the same floor. I already know the cons to this if it doesn't work out. For once I'm channeling my inner positive Petunia and hoping this date is the first of many.

"Is he cute?" Essie asks.

"He's really cute. He's also friends with Brody." I figure that's a safe tidbit.

Essie's eyes light up. "Brody is so sweet! Does that mean Chase plays hockey?"

"He's a forward."

"Oh my God! Oh wow! Look at you go, hooking yourself a hot hockey player. Those guys have endless stamina. At least that's what Rix has said, and I believe it with the way she's always taking Epsom salt baths after Tristan's been on an away series."

"That's probably more information than Rix wants me to have about her sex life." She and Essie were always the queens of the overshare. I used to eavesdrop on their conversations when they were in high school. I learned a lot from their excessively detailed chats.

Essie waves a dismissive hand. "She won't care. I wish I could high-five you! This is awesome!" She flicks her ponytail over her shoulder. "Okay, time's ticking. Let's get you dressed for maximum hotness. Where are you going and what are you doing?"

"We're going for dinner and a movie. And we're university students, so I assume it will be more pub style than fine dining," I say.

"You're probably right. Okay, so black wide-leg pants or jeans are a good start, and a fitted shirt with a hint of cleavage, or tights and that short velvet dress I gave you last Christmas," Essie instructs.

I rummage through my closet and toss clothes on my bed. I change three times—including my bra because Essie claims feeling sexy starts with what you're wearing under your clothes —and we finally settle on an outfit. I want to bring a hoodie but Essie axes that idea. I'm allowed to wear a bomber jacket though, so I don't freeze my ass off.

Next is a quick makeup tutorial. Essie is blissfully easy on me and does not make me attempt cat eyes. Mostly it's a little blush, mascara, shimmer eyeliner to make my grays pop, and gloss to draw attention to my mouth.

"Have the best time!" Essie is all smiles.

"I will, thanks for the help."

"Always my pleasure. And I need to come to campus with Rix one of these days so we can grab lunch. With Tally too because you've been holding out on me, you little sneak. I can't believe you met her without me introducing you. It's a small world, little sister. I'll text you dates soon for all of us to get together."

"I'd love that." And I mean it. I actually think it would be fun to hang out with my sister and our mutual friends.

We blow each other kisses and I end the call. I lace up my

Docs, slide my phone and wallet into my pocket, fluff my hair, and leave my room. It's just my luck that Barbie and Annabelle are walking down the hall when I knock on Chase's door.

"Aww. Isn't that cute. The little weirdo is all dressed up," Annabelle whispers loudly to Barbie.

Chase's door swings open. I swear all the air is sucked out of the universe. He looks magnificent. Hair styled, freshly shaved, dressed in jeans and a long-sleeve collared shirt. His own bomber jacket thrown over top. He's completed the look with a pair of sweet running shoes.

"Hi, Chase!" Annabelle and Barbie say in unison.

He lifts a hand in their direction but doesn't look their way. A smile spreads across his gorgeous face as his eyes rove over me on a slow, hot sweep. "Wow. Hey. Hi. You look amazing."

"Thanks." My stomach flips around at the compliment, and I allow my own gaze to do a slow sweep. "I'd let you fuck my face."

Chase's grin widens.

I slap a palm over my mouth when I notice Brody sitting in his computer chair on the other side of the room. He looks just as comical as Chase did sitting in mine, his huge body making it appear better suited for a child. I glance over my shoulder. It's bad enough Brody heard me. It would be just my luck that the mean girls would overhear that comment and label me the floor slut. Thankfully, Barbie and Annabelle are at the other end of the hall whispering furiously to each other.

Brody spins around in his chair. "Let him take you for dinner and a movie first."

"Hi, Brody," I choke out the words.

"Hi, Cammie." He waves, expression wry as he adds, "And get yours first."

I give him two thumbs-up. "Solid advice."

"Later, Brodes." Chase grabs his phone from his desk and slips it in his pocket.

"Have fun, kids. And play safe." Brody salutes us.

Chase steps into the hall and pulls the door closed behind him.

"He won't say anything to anyone about the face-fuck comment, will he?" We're connected by too many threads and I don't want it to get back to my sister. Not because I think she'll judge me, but because I'm good with having some TMI boundaries with her.

"Nah. He's a vault." Chase laces our fingers and leads me down the hall. "Our ride will be here in like two."

"Where are we headed?"

"There's this cool farm-to-table restaurant downtown. They have a nice menu and even vegan options," Chase explains. "My sister doesn't eat things with faces, so we always go to places that have something for everyone on the carnivore-to-veggie spectrum."

I smile up at him. "That's so thoughtful."

We take the stairs because there's a gaggle of people waiting for the elevator. People say hi to Chase as we push through the doors and step out into the cold, dark November evening. The Uber is already there, so we hop in and take the short trip downtown.

The restaurant is cozy and much nicer than any of the places close to campus. The host tucks us into a booth. Instead of sitting across from me, Chase slides into the seat beside mine. The server is a hipster-looking dude with a bushy beard. We both order ginger ale and flip our menus open.

"I'm starving," Chase says.

"I feel like those are words that come out of your mouth often." I peruse the appetizers. They have fried brussels sprouts, which are a personal fave.

"Yeah, like ninety percent of the time," Chase agrees. "How do you feel about brussels sprouts?"

"Is that a trick question?"

"No. Should it be?"

I shrug. "Depends on your affinity for tiny cabbages."

"I like them. Especially when they're deep fried and served with bacon and tossed in a maple balsamic glaze."

I grin. "I also like them. Especially when they're presented as described."

"Should we start with those?"

"Sure."

When the server returns with our ginger ales, Chase orders the brussels sprouts, the artichoke and spinach dip, and the sausage chips.

"Sausage chips?" I ask when the server disappears.

"Delicious," Chase informs me.

I prop my cheek on my fist. "Better than my precious?"

"No. Nothing tastes better than your precious." His gaze darkens and drops to my mouth. "Except maybe your lips."

I bite the bottom one.

He groans and stretches his arm across the back of the seat. Leaning in, he captures my bottom lip between his and sucks gently. He backs off with a sigh. "We need to talk about literally anything else. Why are you double majoring?"

I stop torturing us and switch gears. "Because a degree in English is nice, but the job opportunities aren't as plentiful as they are with a kinesiology degree. I'll probably go directly into a master's program when I'm done. What about you? Is your goal to make the pros?"

"Ideally, yes. I've been drafted, but that doesn't mean I'll ever get called up. It just depends on how well I'm able to balance the demands of school, hockey, and everything else." Chase traces circles on my shoulder while he talks. "And if I can improve my skill set between now and the end of my time here."

"That seems like a ton of pressure. I don't even have a part-time job and I find the balance between schoolwork and the social stuff hard enough to handle. I can't imagine how challenging it is with hockey basically seven days a week," I muse.

Chase shrugs. "It's my passion. Kind of like writing is yours. You do it because you love it."

"And I love the feedback." Sometimes people leave shitty reviews, but most of the time they have nice things to say. It can be a confidence booster, and it's addictive.

"It's not so different from hockey, apart from the physicality. I love the game and there's a thrill from having all those people cheering you on."

"I can see that." I nod thoughtfully. "But it must get a little old when everyone wants a piece of you."

He fingers the end of my braid. "Not going to lie, it was fun at first, but it got old really fast. I started to feel like a cardboard cutout. Everything felt hollow, if that makes sense." His blue gaze meets mine. "And then there you were."

"I was always there."

"I wasn't ready for you yet."

"And you think you are now?"

"Yeah. Definitely."

The server arrives with our appetizers. We place our dinner orders and dig in.

"These are to die for," I mumble around a mouthful of brussels sprout.

"Right?" Chase pops another one into his mouth.

We chat through dinner—about classes, goals, and our families. It's wild how we're connected through all these hockey people. He tells me stories about how his brother's car got covered in sticky notes last week and how his sister created a peanut butter and jelly sandwich as an oil painting just for fun one year for his dad's birthday. He also asks me about my favorite comfort foods and what I daydream about. Having his undivided attention makes me giddy.

Chase polishes off all the appetizers and finishes what I can't. When I try to go halves with him, he covers my hand with his. "I literally hoovered seventy-five percent of the food we ordered and finished what would have been some nice leftovers for you. I have no expectations beyond this. I'd just like to pay if that's okay with you."

"Okay. Thanks."

He hands over his debit card and once the bill is settled, we head out into the brisk cool night.

"Crap." Chase runs a hand through his hair and his expression turns apologetic. "The movie started almost an hour ago. I didn't realize we'd been at the restaurant this long."

I shove my hands in my jacket pockets. "It's okay. I've seen *The Hobbit* a bunch of times." Like over a hundred. "We can do something else."

Chase consults his phone. "One of the guys on my team is throwing a party tonight. It's only a couple of blocks away. We could go for a bit. I think Brody, Mac, and Gage will be there, so you'll know people and I can introduce you to my other friends?" He chews on the inside of his lip and gives me puppy-dog eyes.

I splay my hand over his face. "That expression is completely unfair."

He takes my hand in his and kisses my palm, batting his long, pretty lashes. "Please, Cammie? I want you to meet my teammates. It'll be fun. We don't have to stay long."

I've never gone to an off-campus party. Essie would be so proud of me. "Okay. We can go to the party."

CHAPTER 17

CHASE

"This house is huge." Cammie steps over an empty beer can and climbs the stairs of the front porch.

"Yeah. One of the guys who lives here is loaded. Well, his parents are loaded. So they bought him this house." He's a decent hockey player, but not pro material. He enjoys the perks of being on the school team and spends more time partying than he does attending classes. He's been on academic probation for the past two years. Apparently, his parents regularly make donations and he keeps getting second chances. My friend Mac also lives with him. The only things the two of them have in common are their mutual love of hockey and a good party.

"Loooovvvvvvett!" One of my teammates slams his body into mine the second we walk through the front door.

I let go of Cammie's hand and shove Docker back. "Dude! The fuck? You almost crushed my girl." I put a protective arm around her.

Docker weaves and blinks blearily at Cammie. "Sorry. Didn't see you there. You're tiny, aren't you?" He pats her on the head.

I smack his hand away. "Don't touch."

Docker raises both hands. "Sorry, man, sorry."

"Are Stiles, Steele, and Meyers around?" I scan the living room.

There's a keg in the middle of the room and some guy I don't know with Freshman written across his forehead in black Sharpie is manning it. Girls in skirts and crop tops lean against walls, talking to each other and some of my teammates.

"Last time I saw them they were out back." Docker thumbs over his shoulder.

"Cool. Thanks." I keep my arm around Cammie's shoulder and lead her through the living room, down the hall, past the kitchen, which is full of people doing shots, and out into the backyard. There's a fire raging in the pit. I'm unsurprised to find Brody slouched in one of the chairs, a red plastic cup in his hand.

"Can I get you a drink?" I have to shout over the music. We're standing under a speaker. I shuffle us away from it and bend until my ear is at her lips.

"I don't drink beer," she shouts.

"There's a cooler out here with the good stuff for the team. We could check it out. See if there's something you want?"

"Sure."

We're stopped five times on the way to the cooler, twice by teammates, and three times by girls who come to our games. I attempt to introduce Cammie, but I don't always remember the girls' names. And I don't want to be rude by asking, so mostly I just let them talk about hockey and the next party before they move on to the next player.

"You really know everyone, don't you?" Cammie muses.

"There are a lot of hockey parties," I explain.

"Yeah, seems like it." She stuffs her free hand in her jacket pocket.

We finally reach the cooler.

"Lovett. How's it hanging?" Beans holds his hand out for a fist bump.

"Long and to the right." I knock his fist. "Beans, this is my girl, Cammie. Cammie, this is Beans. He's an enforcer."

"Hi, Beans." She bumps his fist. "I don't know what an enforcer is, but judging from the size of you, I'm guessing you enforce…something."

Beans laughs. "You're fucking hilarious." He turns to me. "She's hilarious. And cute. Keep an eye on her."

"She's pretty good at taking care of herself." I hug her tightly to my side.

She gives me an arched brow that makes my dick feel things.

Beans gives her a doubtful look. "What can I get you? We have wine, hard seltzer, cider, shots, and pop and water if you're riding the edibles train."

"I'll take a seltzer, please."

Beans passes her a can. I grab a beer, and we make our way over to Brody.

He frowns when he sees us. "I thought you were going to the movies."

"Dinner took longer than expected," I explain.

His frown deepens. "So you came here?"

"Yeah. I wanted to introduce Cammie to our teammates." I give her a squeeze.

She smiles but it doesn't look super convincing. "Do you know where the bathroom is?"

"Yeah. Through the sliding door, down the hall, first door on your left." I point toward the house.

"Can you hold this?" She passes me her drink.

"For sure."

"I'll be back." She kisses me on the cheek. "It's nice to see you, Brody."

"You too, Cammie."

I watch her walk across the lawn, hands tucked into her pockets. She's so fucking beautiful.

Brody kicks me in the shin as she disappears inside the house.

"Ow. What the hell?"

Brody gives me his famous dad look. Sometimes I swear he's channeling his inner fifty-year-old. "What the fuck, bro?"

"What the fuck, what?"

"Why would you bring Cammie to a hockey party?"

"I already told you. Dinner went long and we missed the movie."

He stares at me.

I stare back.

"I wanted to introduce her to our teammates." I've already said this.

"Well, good fucking job, buddy. She's in there by herself with them." He flings a hand in the direction of the house. "I'm sure they'll be more than happy to introduce their drunk asses to her boobs."

I grab the front of his shirt. "Why are you looking at her boobs?"

"I'm not looking at her boobs. She's dressed to highlight her assets. For *you*, dumbass. Because you took her out on a date to spend time with *her*. And then you brought her *here*." He glances at my fist, which is still gripping his shirt.

I release him. "You think it was a bad idea."

"It's your first date and you're choosing to end it at a party."

We have another stare-down.

He connects the dots because I'm apparently an idiot. "Where everyone comes to hook up."

"Shit." I straighten and poke my cheek with my tongue. "Why are you here? Is this some kind of penance?"

"Gage was already half lit when he came up with the amazing idea. I don't want him to get pass-out drunk and not make it to practice in the morning because then he won't be able to play on Saturday and we need him. Of course, Mac disappeared a half hour ago and left me babysitting."

"That makes sense." And it's a total Brody thing to do. And also, a Mac thing.

A girl I vaguely recognize drops into Brody's lap and shrieks his name. She throws her arms around his neck. He looks like he'd rather be hugged by a grizzly bear.

"Are we finally going to hook up tonight?" she whines.

He tips his head back and cups her chin in his palm. "Sweetheart, you don't want to hook up with me. I'm not the good time you're looking for."

She pouts. "You're not?"

He shakes his head. "Now, you know my friend Gage?"

"The tall guy with the dark curly hair?" she asks.

"That's the one. He'll treat you right. I think he's inside. You can tell him I sent you."

"Okay." She hugs him, hops off his lap, and stumble-runs toward the house.

"What the fuck was that?"

"I don't even know." He inclines his head toward the door. "Your girl might need saving."

I follow his gaze. And a growl rips up my throat. Dougie, a second year and the douchiest guy on the team, is leaning against the sliding door, preventing Cammie from leaving the house. She looks uncertain and like he's the last guy she wants to talk to.

"You're so fucked." Brody laughs. "Now go. And get her the fuck out of here. There are better places for her to meet our teammates."

"See you later."

"Hopefully not until tomorrow."

I stalk across the lawn and shout, "Kitten, I have your drink!"

Cammie's eyebrow lifts.

Dougie glances over his shoulder and frowns.

Cammie ducks under his arm and heads for me, mouthing, *kitten*?

But before she reaches me, some girl I've previously hooked up with comes rushing at me out of nowhere and throws her arms around me. Cammie's drink hits the ground and splashes my jeans. Cammie stops halfway across the lawn, and the look on her face reinforces Brody's assertion that this was not the best place to bring her. I extricate myself from the girl who seems to have eight arms instead of two and tell her I have to go, closing the distance between me and Cammie.

I feel like I've fucked this night up epically.

"Wanna get out of here?"

She bites the corner of her lip. "Yeah. That'd be good."

CHAPTER 18

CAMMIE

I shrug off Chase's arm when he tries to put it around my shoulder and stuff my hands in my pockets. I'm positive that girl who practically glued herself to him a minute ago is a former hookup. She was so thrilled to see him, and then she shot daggers at me with her pretty, green eyeballs when he basically shrugged her off, exactly like I've done to Chase.

I'm so out of my depth. What started as a great night has done a swan dive into a pile of crap. I'm grateful when Chase doesn't suggest walking through the house again and guides me around the outside. I feel horribly out of place, and stupidly jealous.

All these girls who go to these parties are effortlessly cool and pretty and have no problem talking to him. Or any of the other guys. They're fun and fun to be around. They want to be here. And it doesn't matter that I'm standing right beside him. They all seem to look right through me. Like I'm a pane of glass. Like I'm not even there.

"Chase man! You just got here!" A guy calls out.

"Chase! I didn't even get to say hi!" Another freaking girl rushes over and throws her arms around him.

"My girl has an early class. I'll see you later." He extracts himself from her hug and rushes to catch up to me.

I know this neighborhood. We're not that far from campus. It's maybe a fifteen-minute walk. I just need to hold it together that long.

As I head for the sidewalk, the front door is thrown open and two girls rush out. Two familiar girls. Barbie and Annabelle.

"You were supposed to be keeping guard!" Barbie barks at Annabelle.

"I didn't know you were going to take his jersey!" Annabelle tries to get her to stop. "You have to give it back!"

"Not now!" Barbie snaps her fingers at Annabelle. "Come on, let's get out of here."

Annabelle looks like the last thing she wants to do is follow Barbie, but she does anyway, and they disappear down the street at a sprint.

"That looked intense," Chase mutters.

I head down the sidewalk going in the same direction as Annabelle and Barbie, but they've already disappeared around the corner. Chase falls into step beside me.

"Cammie."

I make a noise, but don't say anything.

Chase tugs on the sleeve of my jacket. "Hey. Are you okay? Did Dougie say something to you?"

"I'm fine." Dougie was annoyingly stereotypical. He asked who I came with. When I said Chase, he laughed like he didn't believe me. Sure, he was drunk, but that's when people's filters disappear. He was just speaking his drunken truth.

"You're not fine. Can you stop for a second? Please."

We're far enough away from Mac's house and between streetlamps, so no one can witness this. I better not cry. I bite my lips together.

"Tell me what's wrong? What happened?"

"Did you hook up with that girl who hugged you?" The question is out before I can call it back.

"Which one?" He cringes and his expression shifts to discomfort. "Do you really want to know?"

I sigh and tip my head back. "Not really, and that basically answers the question anyway." It's a pretty night. There are stars in the sky and the moon is bright. How different would this have been if we'd made it to the movie? "I don't know if this is a good idea." Or if my heart can handle being broken by Chase.

His brows pull together in a delicious furrow. It's so unfair that he can be pretty even when he's displeased.

"What's not a good idea?"

I swallow past the lump in my throat and motion between us. "This." God, my feelings are too big, and the look on his face is ruining me.

"Because that girl hugged me?" He shoves his hand through his hair, like he's just as anxious as me.

"No. Not because she hugged you. I mean, it's part of it. I don't look like any of the girls at these parties, Chase. I'm not cool, it's not really my scene and it's definitely yours." There's a huge lump clogging my throat.

"First of all, you're beautiful, Cammie. Second, you're the coolest fucking person I know."

I give him a look.

"I'm serious. And just because this hasn't been your scene doesn't mean you won't ever like a party," Chase implores. "I thought maybe it would be a good way for you to meet my friends, but I realize now maybe it was a bit overwhelming."

"I'm scared, Chase," I admit.

"Of what? Talk to me, Cammie. I can't fix this if I don't know what I did wrong."

If I'm not honest we'll never get anywhere. And how will I feel if I let my fears rule me? What will keeping this to myself solve? Nothing. I motion toward Mac's house. "All those girls in there are so different from me. Besides being put together and pretty and cool, they don't have a problem coming up to you and saying hi, or even hugging you. Even when I was standing right there."

"I don't need you to be like those girls. I like you just the way you are."

"That's not really the point, though. It's fine when it's just the two of us. But when we're with your friends I don't feel… included. I disappear to you just like I do with all of them. You didn't introduce me to half the people who said hi to you," I explain.

"I didn't remember their names," he admits.

"Is that supposed to make me feel better? Because honestly, it really doesn't."

He nods slowly, maybe absorbing my words. "I can see why that would be problematic." He rubs his bottom lip with his thumb. "I'm sorry I brought you here."

"I don't want you to be sorry for bringing me to a party, Chase. I can see how they could be fun. I just need you to remember to try to include me." I shore up my courage to say the last part, because it's the hardest to verbalize. "I just want to feel as special when we're out together as I do when we're alone."

His breath leaves him on a whoosh, and he steps in and cups my face in his cold palms. "You are special. So special. You're the only girl I've ever felt this way about." He presses his forehead to mine. "Give me a chance, please? I'm new at this, and clearly not great at the whole boyfriend thing, but I can learn. I want to learn. I want to be a good boyfriend. More than that, I want to be your boyfriend."

My heart stutters and gallops. "I want you to be my boyfriend, too," I whisper.

He wraps me in his warm, strong arms and buries his face against my neck. "I'll do better next time, I promise. And if I'm fucking shit up, please call me out. I don't want to lose you." He pulls back and brushes his lips over mine.

"I don't want to lose you either."

CHAPTER 19

CHASE

"Hop on, I'll piggyback you the rest of the way."

"You don't have to carry me," Cammie assures me.

"I want to, though." And I want to get back so I can make up for being a clueless fucking idiot. Of course, Cammie felt awkward and left out at that party. If I went to a *LotR* event I'm sure I'd feel like a total fish out of water. I want her to feel comfortable with my friends. And while I can't rewind tonight, I can think of a few ways to remind her how good we are together, and that I can learn how to be the best fucking boyfriend in the damn world.

She climbs up onto my back and I hook my arms under her knees. She wraps hers around my shoulders and rests her cheek against my neck. I pick up the pace.

"Are you carrying me because I wasn't walking fast enough?"

"No. I just want to get back to res."

Her nose brushes the shell of my ear. "What happens when we get back to res?"

"Whatever you want to happen." I turn my head and her lips brush my cheek.

I feel her smile. "Does that mean you want dessert?"

"Only if you think I deserve it."

"I think my pussy deserves it," she murmurs.

"Fuck, yes please." I stumble over a curb, but don't lose my footing.

Cammie laughs and holds tighter.

I don't put her down until we're in the elevator on the way up to the third floor. "I'm really sorry about the party."

"I know." The elevator doors slide open and we link fingers. Cammie unlocks the door to her room and holds it open for me.

She flicks on her light and we both stand there, staring at each other. I let her take the lead on this, just in case she's not where I am right now.

"Did you finish reading my chapter last night?" she asks.

"I actually went back to the beginning and read everything *but* the newest chapter because Brody came home," I admit. "It was so fucking hot. I really destroyed that cloth you gave me."

She shrugs out of her jacket and jiggles her mouse so the computer screen comes to life. "Do you want to finish reading it now?"

"Please, yes. I would love that."

She taps the computer chair.

I throw myself into it and pat my thighs. "You'll sit with me again?"

A coy smile turns up the corner of her plush lips. "Sure."

She settles her luscious ass in my lap and I roll us closer to her desk so she can pull up the chapter.

She glances over her shoulder. "Are you already hard?"

"Between you being sexy as fuck and your words being hot as fuck, I'm hard as fuck."

She smiles and pulls up her story. "Do you want to start where you left off?"

"Maybe the beginning of the chapter, just so I get the full effect?" I wrap an arm around her waist and nuzzle through her hair so I can kiss her neck.

She scrolls to the beginning of the chapter I started last night and I scan the page, refamiliarizing myself with the characters and the story. I slide a hand under her shirt as Aragorn does the same.

Cammie makes a little noise in the back of her throat to match Arwen. I take her lobe between my teeth, biting gently. "Can I take your shirt off?"

"Didn't you say you were bad at multitasking?"

"I can't get better at it if I don't try," I bargain.

She raises her hands over her head and I remove her shirt. Her bra is black and lacy and so fucking sexy. I kiss along her bare shoulder.

Cammie raps her nails on the desk. "Keep reading."

"Right. Yes." I drag my eyes back to the screen and cup Cammie's breast as Aragorn does the same to Arwen. Legolas is behind her, unclasping her bra and kissing her neck while Aragorn kisses a path down her stomach.

"You can take my bra off too, if you want," Cammie offers.

She sits forward and I flick it open, and the black straps slide down her arms. I cup her perfect, perky, lush tits and brush my thumbs over her nipples. Cammie arches as they harden under my touch.

I keep reading as Aragorn and Legolas devote their attention to Arwen, kissing and touching as they undress each other.

"You should take your shirt off, too," Cammie suggests breathlessly.

I whip it over my head and she sighs as her warm back meets my hard chest.

She moves one hand to the waistband of her pants. "I want you to touch me."

"You want me to touch you where?" I ask, clarifying. My cock is so fucking hard, and Cammie keeps shifting around in my lap, rubbing her ass on my erection.

"My pussy, please," she whispers.

She doesn't have to ask twice. I pop the button on her jeans.

"Can I take these off to make it easier?" Cammie naked in my lap? Yes, fucking please.

She grips the armrests and lifts enough that I can push her jeans and black lace panties over her hips and down her thighs. She kicks them off and settles back in my lap.

I run my hands down her thighs and push her knees apart. "Hook your feet around my calves," I instruct.

Cammie adjusts her position so she's spread for me and my palms glide back up the inside of her thighs, thumbs sweeping along the edge of her pussy. She whimpers and grips the armrests.

Aragorn and Legolas lay Arwen on the bed and shower her body with kisses. I skim her clit as Aragorn buries his face between her thighs. When he slides a finger into Arwen, I do the same to Cammie.

"You're so fucking beautiful," I murmur in her ear, adding a second finger, pumping into her soft wetness. "I can't wait to taste you again."

Cammie tugs on my hand between her thighs. "Give me your fingers."

I reluctantly do as she asks, then almost cream in my fucking pants when she drags my pussy-juice-soaked index finger along her bottom lip, shoves her hand into my hair, twists my head, and offers me her mouth.

I suck her bottom lip and slide my fingers back inside her. Cammie arches, ass pressing against my erection. I cup her cheek and explore her mouth with my tongue, while I finger-fuck her to the same rhythm. She moans into my mouth, shuddering her way through an orgasm.

When she melts into me, I bite the edge of her jaw. "Stop being so enticing for a hot second so I can finish this chapter."

She laughs and rests her head against my shoulder, cheek against my neck.

"Oh fuck," I mutter as I get to the part where Arwen sits on

Aragorn's face and she fists both their cocks. And then blows them. "This is hot as hell," I groan, scrolling with shaky hands as Arwen gets tag-teamed and really, really seems to love it.

I'm panting by the time I've finished the chapter. I grip Cammie by the waist and carry her over to her bed. It's a twin, and stupidly small compared to the hotel king, but I'm desperate for the taste of her on my tongue. I lay her out on the bed, drag her to the edge by her ankles, sink to my knees, and bury my face in her pussy. She pulls a pillow over her face to muffle her moans. I make her come again and I feel like a fucking god.

I stand and she sits up, legs bracketing mine as she fumbles with my belt. "You don't have to," I grind out.

She arches a brow. "Oh, but Chase, I *want* to."

She frees my erection, her delicate, warm, soft fingers wrapping around my shaft. She gives it a slow stroke and nuzzles it, eyes closing as she rubs it on her cheek. It's weeping already.

Her gaze lifts to mine as she drags her tongue through the slit and presses a soft kiss to the tip. "I want you to fuck my mouth again." She brushes her lips back and forth over the head.

My cock kicks in her hand. "Like last time?"

She nods and wraps her lips around the head, applying suction.

"I want to try something, but you tell me if it doesn't work for you, okay?"

Her eyes light up with excitement that makes my dick even harder. "Okay. How do you want me?"

That's a loaded fucking question. I want her hard and fast, soft and slow, and every way in between. But one step at a time.

I tap the end of the mattress. "I want your head right here, Cammie."

She lies down on the bed, gloriously naked, the top of her head at my thighs. I adjust her so her head is almost hanging off the bed. I cup her head in my hand, supporting her so she doesn't have to strain her neck. One shin is braced against the edge of the bed, the other knee rests on the mattress beside her head. She takes me in her hand and guides me to her mouth. As soon as her lips cover the crown, she releases me.

Cammie tips her head back, opening wider, and I slide in a couple of inches. The view is fucking incredible even if the position requires more focus on my part. But I have a plan and excellent thigh strength. And Cammie is a fucking adventure in bed, so we can probably make this work.

"This okay?" I grind out.

She mumbles an affirmative with a mouth full of cock. I carefully support her head and guide her mouth with one hand while I brush a thumb over her nipple with the free one. Cammie moans and grabs her other breast, squeezing aggressively.

I have a plan though, and I'm hoping like fuck I can execute it, because if it works it'll be hot as fuck. Cammie is small, I'm tall, so in theory it should be doable. I adjust my grip on the back of her head, making sure it's secure before I slide my hand down her stomach and dip between her legs. I'm rewarded with another moan.

She grabs my leg as I slide a single finger inside her and tips her head back further, taking another inch of cock. I add another finger. She moans and digs her fingers into my leg. I pull my hips back until the head appears. "Is this okay?"

"Yes please, more," she pants.

"You're a fucking miracle, Cammie." She's a fucking vision. Cammie's head balanced in my palm as I fuck her mouth, my fingers buried in her tight, sweet pussy. Her legs start to shake, and she moans her way through an orgasm. I remove my fingers, pull out of her mouth, and quickly reposition myself so I'm straddling her torso. Cammie slides down the bed and props herself on her elbows. I hold her head and slide back inside.

"I'm going to come soon," I warn.

And just like last time, she grabs my ass and pulls me deep. Her wide eyes lock on mine, full of primal satisfaction.

The orgasm slams through me and I groan her name, long

and loud…probably louder than I should. I carefully pull out and rearrange us on the bed so she's lying on my chest. "Can I stay in your room tonight?"

Cammie kisses the edge of my jaw. "Yeah, you can sleep over."

I'm pretty sure I'm already falling for her.

CHAPTER 20

CAMMIE

I'm supposed to be writing my English paper. And finishing the creative writing submission with the looming deadline that's creeping up on me like a bad wedgie. It's amazing how time speeds up when things are due and all those weeks I had disappear one at a time. Since Chase became my boyfriend I've been to a couple of hockey parties. They're still a little overwhelming, but I'm getting to know his teammates, and he's been a lot better about making sure I feel included.

Tonight we're studying, though. Or we're supposed to be. But Chase is lying on my bed, shirtless, wearing black joggers, with his biology textbook propped on his glorious abs. So I obviously started a chapter about Arwen seducing Aragorn as he was trying to decode an ancient scroll while Legolas was out hunting for dinner.

Chase is deeply focused on his textbook. Occasionally uncapping his highlighter with his teeth and marking an important passage. I've learned over the past few weeks that Chase is passionate about hockey, school, and my vagina. He's smart and nerds out over anything science related. And he's so hot it should be illegal. He's also exceptionally good at giving me orgasms and looks unbelievably sexy when he's focused on making me feel good. Every time I look at him, my pulse races, and my stomach twists in the most incredible way.

I roll my chair back. Chase continues to study like the good boy he is. I pull my shirt over my head and unclasp my bra. He continues to read, lips moving while he scans the page. I shove my jogging pants and underwear down my legs. He still doesn't notice. I cross over to the bed and straddle his hips.

He startles and his eyes go wide. "Holy fuck." He tosses his textbook on the floor, gaze raking over my naked form on a hot sweep.

"Hi."

His wide, warm palms glide up my thighs. "You're naked."

"I was hot." I smooth my hands over his bare chest.

"You sure fucking are." His fingers skim the edge of my jaw, sending a shiver down my spine as his palm curves around the back of my neck and he pulls my mouth to his.

Mission Seduce Chase accomplished. Before he and I were forced together as unlikely roommates, there wasn't a chance in hell that I'd ever get naked in a fully lit room to get my boyfriend's attention. But Chase makes me feel like the sexiest woman on the planet.

He quickly flips us over and settles in the cradle of my hips. He props himself up on one elbow, hand still cradling my head while we make out and I roll my hips. Eventually he breaks the kiss. "I'm going to go say hi to precious for a little while, okay?"

I nod. "Yes, please, we'd love that."

His grin turns downright lascivious as he kisses a path over my chest, stopping at my nipples, before he goes lower. His broad shoulders nudge my legs apart and he licks me, groaning as he sucks my clit. I run my hands through his thick hair and grip the strands as I cant my hips. Even though there's music playing in the background, I shove a pillow over my face when the orgasm hits to muffle my moans.

Chase kisses his way back up my body and I wrap myself around him, exploring his mouth, turned on by the taste of myself on his tongue. I push his joggers over his hips to free his erection and the shaft slides over my clit.

"Ah fuck." Chase buries his face against my neck. "You feel so fucking good, Cammie." He gently bites his way along my jaw to my lips. "So hot and soft and wet."

I tip my hips on his next roll and he slides low, the blunt head pressing against my opening. I moan and tighten my legs around his waist. He pushes up on his arm, questions in his eyes.

His thumb sweeps along the side of my neck. "Cammie, baby?"

I clench at the pet name. "I want to if you want to," I whisper, suddenly really fucking nervous.

His expression softens as he brushes his lips over mine. "There's no pressure, okay? It's whenever you're ready."

"I am." I lick my lips. "I'm ready." And I mean it. I want this with Chase. He always takes care of me, makes sure I come, that I feel good, that I'm comfortable with the things we try. Sometimes they don't work and we end up laughing, but most of the time it's hot and a little dirty and I love it. I'm definitely falling for him. And there's nothing more intimate than allowing him into my body.

"You're sure?" His cock twitches.

"I'm sure." I run my fingers through his hair and swallow thickly.

He tips his head. "I promise it's okay if you're not. I'll wait as long as you need me to."

"I know." I bite the inside of my cheek. I just need to spit it out. "I haven't before."

His brow furrows, then shoots up. "Haven't as in..." He lets it hang.

"I haven't had sex before."

His breath leaves him on a whoosh. "You're a virgin?"

I bite my lips together and nod. What if he rejects me? What if he says no? What if he doesn't want me?

He lifts his hips and adjusts his position, shaft gliding over my clit. He takes my face in his hands and presses his lips gently to mine. "Are you sure this is how you want this to happen? I could take you to a hotel, get champagne and rose petals. It should be special, Cammie."

"It's you. It will be special." I finger an errant curl at the nape of his neck. "A hotel and all those things just sound like too much pressure. I want it to be here, where I'm comfortable."

He gazes down at me, expression intense. "You're sure you don't want rose petals and a king bed?"

"I'm sure. We're here now."

"Okay." He brushes his lips over mine. "Let me just grab a condom."

"There are a couple in the nightstand. They came in the welcome bag from the health center." I don't know why I feel the need to explain when I've just told him it's my first time.

He gazes down at me, and I look up at him.

His swallow is audible. "I have better ones."

"Are they ribbed for my pleasure?" I ask, mostly joking.

"Not quite." He gives me a quick kiss, rolls off me, and rummages around in his backpack until he finds his wallet.

I lie on the bed trying to figure out what's so special about his condoms while staring at his magnificent ass. I'm about to lose my virginity. This is a huge deal. The biggest deal of my freshman year in university.

Chase spins around. His massive cock sticks out like a divining rod. He's holding a green foil packet in his hand. He takes one look at me and crosses back over to the bed. "Are you okay?"

"Yeah. Good. Great. Awesome." The pitch of my voice belies the lie.

He sits down next to me, expression serious. It would be easier to handle if his giant cock wasn't straining next to my elbow. "We don't have to."

I close my legs. "I know. I want to."

"It might hurt at first." He seems really displeased by this possibility.

I nod. "There's a good chance. Even with my limited experience I'm highly aware you have a really big dick."

He doesn't disagree with me. "We'll go slow. And if you want to stop, we'll stop." He's very emphatic about the last part. Which I appreciate.

"Okay."

He sets the condom on the nightstand and stretches out beside me. "Let me get you ready."

"Shouldn't I already be ready?"

"You can never have enough foreplay." He kisses me and trails his fingers down my stomach. He teases me with a gentle touch that lights me up and keeps me on edge, but never tips me over. Eventually he fits himself between my thighs and we make out, grinding against each other until I'm begging him for more.

Chase grabs the condom from the nightstand and I watch as he tears it open and pinches the tip, taking mental notes as he rolls it down his generous length. He stretches out over me and his erection rubs against me. Chase cups my cheek in his warm palm and his hot gaze locks on mine.

"Tell me what you want, Cammie." His thumb brushes along the edge of my jaw.

"I want this first with you."

His eyes fall closed and his forehead rests against mine.

For a very long few seconds, I'm terrified that he's going to back out.

But he lifts his head, determination and something else I can't quite identify crossing his face. "I'll go slow."

"Okay."

He reaches between us and lines himself up, the blunt tip

nudging my entrance this time. Chase's gaze stays locked on my face as he pushes in just a bit.

"You okay, baby?"

"I'm okay." I grip his shoulders and try to relax my breathing, but I'm so nervous. What if I can't handle it? What if I'm terrible at sex? What if I'm too loud? Or not loud enough?

He pushes in a bit more and I tense.

"Just relax." He covers my mouth with his.

I try.

He pushes in another inch. This time it's accompanied with a burning sensation. I clamp my legs against his hips.

"I should stop. We should stop."

But I don't want to stop. I want this. People wouldn't have sex all the time if it didn't feel good. My peers wouldn't be looking for endless hookups if it felt awful. I overheard Essie and Rix talking about their firsts and how it wasn't great at first…but then. *Then*.

"Please don't stop."

"Okay." He kisses me. "Okay." His jaw clenches.

He sinks in another inch.

That awful burning intensifies. I try not to let it show on my face, but the little whimper that escapes me is pretty fucking damning.

"We're stopping," Chase states. With authority. With conviction. With uneasy determination.

"We're not." I lock my legs around his waist and tilt my hips up and push down on his ass. And he sinks. Into me. Filling me in one stroke. Bottoming out. The *wild* burn rushes through me and steals my breath. It's a sensation I don't know what to do with. I succumb. But also. *Also*…the fullness, and then…*then*…the pleasurable ache that makes everything tighten.

"Shit. Shit. Fuck." His hands tremble against my cheeks. "Cammie, Cammie, *Cammie*." A full body shudder runs through him, followed by a deep primal groan.

I do this to him. Being inside me like this makes him feel this way.

His jaw tics and his gaze darkens in the most delicious way. Especially since it contrasts with the gentle way he touches me. Fingers brushing along my cheek. "Tell me you're okay." It's as much a plea as a demand.

"I'm okay." It's a raspy croak. "Can we just…stay like this for a minute?"

"Yeah, of course." He kisses me, soft and sweet.

The burn fades and the fullness remains. I swivel my hips, testing out the way it feels. That strange discomfort flares momentarily and fades, something hot and needy taking its place.

Chase gazes down at me, eyes hooded with desire. "How does it feel?"

I swivel my hips again and little jolts of pleasure zip through me. "Good, it feels good."

He rolls his hips and that pleasure sparks.

"Oh God, do that again," I moan.

"Like this?" He repeats the action.

My nails dig into his shoulders and I shift under him. "Yes. Again. Please."

This time he pulls out a bit and pushes back in. There's a moment of discomfort, but it's quickly replaced by pleasure. He starts a gentle rhythm, eyes never leaving mine, hand on my face, body close, arms caging me protectively.

I don't expect an orgasm. Not the first time. But he carefully hooks my leg under his arm and it changes the angle. His pelvis rubs against my sensitive clit with every gentle thrust. Sensation expands, flowing through my veins, turning into a storm in my belly. It takes over and I fall and fly.

"That's it, that's my girl," Chase grinds out. "Look at me, Cammie. Let me see you."

I pry my eyes open and it feels like I'm inside him just like he's inside me. The orgasm is incredible. The most amazing cacophony of sensation and emotions merging.

Chase's brow furrows and his mouth drops open. His hips jerk and he thrusts hard once, twice, a third time. Every muscle locks and his expression is sheer, unbridled euphoria.

He collapses, sweaty and panting, then rolls to the side so he doesn't crush me. He holds me tight and cups my head in his palm, kissing me softly.

"Hi." He brushes my hair away from my face.

"Hi."

"How you doing?"

I grin. "I'm good. How are you?"

"Just good? I thought maybe you came?" He looks so hopeful.

"I did come. And I'm great. At first it was…different, and then it was so, so good. I'd definitely do it again," I assure him.

His answering smile is radiant. "Okay, good. I'm glad."

"Was it good for you?" My gaze drops to his throat.

He tips my chin up. "It was amazing. You're amazing." He kisses me softly.

We lie there for another minute, just kissing and touching before he carefully eases out. There's no blood, but I'm definitely going to be a little sore tomorrow. Not in a bad way, though.

Chase rolls off the bed and grabs his joggers from the floor.

For a moment I'm horrified.

Until he grabs my keycard from my desk. "I'm going to get you a warm damp cloth. I'll be right back." He disappears into the hall.

I lie there trying to decide if I feel different. Maybe a little. Now I know what all the fuss is about, and I have some actual experience to go with the sexy stuff I write and have only imagined before now.

Chase returns a minute later with a warm damp washcloth. He carefully wipes between my legs and presses a soft kiss to my pussy before he grabs his T-shirt from the floor and pulls it over my head. And then he snuggles me to sleep. It's freaking incredible.

In the morning, he kisses me goodbye before he leaves for practice. On my desk is a cafeteria cup filled with wildflowers, a blueberry muffin, and a coffee.

I'm definitely falling for Chase.

And I definitely want to have sex again. Just as soon as my vagina stops having a pulse of its own.

CHAPTER 21

CHASE

"You were on fire on the ice tonight!" Steele chest bumps me while still fully dressed in his gear.

The past week has been awesome. Cammie and I have had sex three times. She needed a couple of recovery days after the first time, but then we had sex two days in a row. Having sex with someone I care about feels different. It's addictive. I want more of her wrapped around me, more of her moaning my name, more of the soft look on her face when she's orgasm happy.

We stayed up way too late talking about her feelings regarding *The Rings of Power* and what her childhood was like. She constantly surprises me, making me laugh about her antics during her martial arts training. I want to know everything about her. I know she hates when it gets really cold. She thinks apple is a superior fall flavor. She wants to be an author but doesn't know if she's brave enough to do it. I think she can do anything though. I'm definitely in deep.

A couple of the fourth-year players ruffle my hair and give me props as they pass me on the way to the showers. It was just a team scrimmage, but we have a game tomorrow night, and I'm hoping I get some good ice time on account of my performance.

"Seriously, nice work out there," Brody says as we strip off our jerseys and start removing our pads.

"Thanks. Scoring a goal felt fantastic." Our goalie is known for shutouts; getting past him is incredible.

"It was seriously kick-ass. I'm sure they'll put you in the game tomorrow night. And we can book extra ice time next week if you want to work on your wrist shot," he offers.

"Yeah. Let's check our schedules." Between assignments, daily practice, and classes, it's hard to find time for anything else. Thankfully the game tomorrow is at home. Games are always on the weekend, and the away ones cut into my Cammie time.

But tonight is a good reminder that I'm here on a hockey scholarship and if I'm really fucking lucky, I could end my four years here with a degree *and* a contract for the pros. Balancing school, a relationship, and hockey is a lot, but I'm up for the challenge.

We hop in the showers and change back into our dress clothes.

Mac slings an arm over each of our shoulders as we make our way through the lobby. "We're going out and you're both coming."

"I'll come for food, but that's it," I say.

"Same," Brody seconds.

"Just because you have a girlfriend doesn't mean you can't have a freaking life, dude," Gage grumbles as he joins us.

"I do have a life," I say defensively. Maybe it's not quite the life I envisioned a few months ago, but my priorities have shifted. And Cammie is hanging out with her friend tonight, so she's busy anyway.

Do I want to sleep alone in my own bed? No. But we have a hard time keeping our hands to ourselves. There's a chance she'd try to seduce me even though she probably needs a night off, so her being out is for the best.

"Dudes, why the hell did we get fake IDs if all you're up for is wings?" Gage pushes between us and picks up the pace so he can join a few of the other guys.

"You know if he goes out, he'll get stupid on shots," Brody mutters.

"He always gets stupid on shots. Like I want to risk ruining my Uber score because he has to ask them to pull over so he can hurl." It's happened before. Thankfully it was on his Uber account, not mine. He showed up to practice the next day hungover and hurled on the ice. He was suspended for two games.

Mac sighs. "I'll watch him tonight. I owe you for that party a while back, Stiles."

Brody doesn't skip a beat. "Hell yeah, you do, bro."

"We could go for like an hour, if Gage still decides he's up for it later?"

Brody gives me a look as we slide into two seats at the end of the table while Mac follows Gage to the other end. "Since when are you one to fold under peer pressure?"

"I just feel like…I don't know. I don't want to bail on him all the time. And maybe like…I'm missing out if I don't?" But honestly, I'd rather be with Cammie than anywhere else.

"Does it feel like you're missing out?" He does this often—throws the question I asked back at me.

"No. But—" I shrug.

"Sorry to interrupt. What can I get you guys to drink?" The server is a pretty brunette.

"I'll have a Coke, please."

"I'll have the same, thanks. And we're ready to order if that's cool," Brody adds.

"Sure thing."

Brody orders our wings and a side of cheesy garlic bread. She moves on to the next guys at the table.

"If it doesn't feel like you're missing out, then what's the issue?"

"I don't know. I'm locking in early, I guess? Earlier than I thought I would." I didn't think I'd have a girlfriend before the end of my first semester. "I guess I figured maybe I'd settle down in fourth year or something."

He nods. "Cammie's cool, though, and she's not clingy. She's got her own thing going on and she's pretty chill."

"Yeah. For sure. She's just like…unapologetically herself, you know?" She's smart, funny, easy to hang out with, and a fucking revelation between the sheets. And we've just started to learn each other.

"She's good for you and you're good for her," he agrees.

"I'm super into her." I glance to my left, making sure no one else is listening as I lean in and lower my voice. "Like I think maybe…she's it." When I think about my future, I see her in it.

Brody rests his forearms on the table and clasps his hands. "If you know, you know."

"But like, I'm not even nineteen yet."

Brody shrugs. "Maybe it feels early because we hang out with guys like Gage who want to fuck their way through their university career. But look at Flint and Jason. Those guys have been with their girlfriends since first year and you don't see them worrying about missing out on shit. They don't have FOMO because they have what they need."

He's right. Flint and Jason are third years. When those guys come to parties they always bring their girlfriends. I haven't had a chance to introduce Cammie to them yet. Hopefully soon, though. They always attend home games and wear their jerseys, cheering Flint and Jason on. "Cammie's what I need."

"So, if she's your person, just own it and be glad you found her now and you don't have to do the heartbreak thing a bunch of times. Gage and those dudes are just noise. Block it out and do what's best for you."

I imagine what the next few years could be like. Cammie and I studying together, hanging out. She can come to my games, give me good luck kisses before I hit the ice. We can have hot celebration sex when our team wins during home games. She'll be the last person I talk to every night, no matter where I am.

The server drops off a huge bucket of wings. Gage pulls up a chair. "You two look way too serious for beer and wings. What's going on?"

"Just talking strategy for our game tomorrow night," Brody lies smoothly.

"We're going to kick Brock U's ass." Gage digs into the bucket of wings.

We talk hockey and eat wings until my stomach hurts. Gage doesn't ask us if we want to try to get into the bar with them when we've polished off all the food. Instead, we head back to campus, along with a few other guys who also bowed out. Brody and I brush our teeth but my mouth annoyingly still tastes like wings. When I'm settled in bed, I send a good-night text to Cammie.

CHASE

How is your night with Tally going?

CAMMIE

We've almost finished our movie marathon.

I check the time. It's after one in the morning.

CHASE

Do you want me to walk over and walk you back?

CAMMIE

That's sweet, but I'll crash here. I'll see you tomorrow, though?

CHASE

We can grab breakfast or something?

CAMMIE

Sounds good. I'll text when I'm awake. Sweet dreams. Xx

CHASE

They're sweetest when you're next to me. See you in the morning. Xx

CHAPTER 22

CAMMIE

Chase wraps his arms around me and picks me up off the ground so my toes bump against his shins. "Hi, I missed you last night."

"I missed you, too." I kiss the side of his neck and inhale. Except I don't get the usual whiff of aftershave. "Do you smell like buffalo sauce?"

"Probably. There were a lot of wings last night and I was in a rush getting out the door to you this morning." He sets me on my feet, sniffs his sweatshirt, and shudders. "I need something healthy to balance out last night's bad choices."

"Did you go somewhere after wings?" I ask. A tiny twinge of unease makes my shoulders tight. I will not be an overbearing girlfriend. I will not let my own insecurities get the best of me.

"Nah, Brody and I came back to the dorms." He laces our fingers and we head into the cafeteria. "Gage went out, though. I seriously hope he didn't get super fucked up. We really need him at tonight's game."

"What position does he play again?" Tally gave me a crash course in hockey last night. She's a wealth of knowledge about the sport.

"He's an enforcer," Chase explains.

"So defense, right? And you're a forward?" I ask.

He smiles down at me. "Yeah, left wing."

"And Brody? What position does he play?"

"He's right wing, but he'll probably be a center. He's strong on the ice and has wicked speed." Chase loads up a bowl with fresh fruit and yogurt and tops it with granola.

I grab the usual: a blueberry muffin. "How was practice last night?"

We stop at the coffee urns and both fill a cup. "Good. Great, actually. I scored a goal."

"That's awesome!" Scoring a goal is hard based on the little hockey I've watched.

"Thanks." He beams.

We use our meal plan cards to pay for breakfast and find a table near the windows.

Chase spears a chunk of pineapple covered in yogurt. "Maybe you want to come to my game tonight?"

I accidentally drop my muffin. Thankfully it lands on my plate.

"Unless you're busy with that creative writing submission. I know the due date is coming up," he tacks on, but I don't miss the disappointment already clouding his eyes.

I should be long finished with my submission, but I'm not, and tonight would be a great time to work on it. It could be another convenient excuse not to go. But Chase is my boyfriend and hockey is his passion. I don't want to be an unsupportive girlfriend. And I can't avoid running into his past hookups forever. "I can come to your game tonight."

His whole face lights up. "Really?"

"Yeah. I'd love to see you play."

I'm a ball of fucking nervous energy as I enter the arena. Alone. Tally is meeting me here, but she had a group study session that ran late, so she'll be another twenty minutes. The game starts in ten. The teams are already on the ice, warming up. The arena is filling up with spectators. I don't want to disappoint Chase by showing up late, but going in there by myself feels a lot like entering the lion's den while wearing a raw meat suit.

Arwen wouldn't back down from the catty girls.

I roll my shoulders back, exhale my anxiety, push through the doors, and inhale the sharp bite of rubberized floor mats and the fresh scent of ice. Music blasts through the sound system, echoing off the high ceilings. My breath puffs out in front of me as I scan the arena for unoccupied seats. I spot three several rows back from the ice in the middle, so I head for those.

Chase gave me a pom-pom toque boasting the university's hockey team to wear. The seats are full of students, and loads of girls are in full makeup, wearing jerseys, team hoodies, toques, and scarves. Apparently, I need to invest in a team hoodie and all the other things if I want to appropriately represent my boyfriend.

I ask the girls at the end of the row if anyone is sitting in the middle. One girl gives me an appraising once-over. "Not that I know of."

"Cool, thanks." I mutter *excuse me* as I shimmy past them, to the three empty seats. I drop into the one in the middle and message Tally to let her know what row I'm in, then survey the ice, looking for Chase.

I spot LOVETT across a set of broad shoulders and the number 19 on the back passing a puck back and forth with STILES as they lap the rink. My stomach flips as they pass me. The buzzer sounds and the team skates to the bench, which is to the right of where I'm seated. A whole bunch of girls wearing team hoodies are congregated in the seats closest to the ice. Two girls are wearing jerseys. I imagine they had to get here pretty early to score those seats. The corresponding players bang their gloves on the plexiglass barrier, giving those girls a chin tip and a wink. They blow kisses.

Maybe those are their girlfriends. I make a mental note to show up earlier. And to learn more of the rules of the game so I know what's going on.

Chase scans the group, maybe looking for me, his gaze lifting higher. I pull the toque on my head as his eyes pass over me a second time and then stop. My cheeks flame as his grin widens. I lift a tentative hand in a wave and he waves back.

"Shut them down tonight, Steele!" someone else shouts and Gage fist-pumps the air and sends a wink in their direction.

"Woohoo! I hope you score a goal tonight, Lovett!" a girl shouts from behind me.

"Show them how it's done!" another girl yells.

I go rigid. I swear I know those voices. I pull my hood up and as covertly as possible, glance over my shoulder. I'm right. Barbie and Annabelle are in the row behind me, down a few seats to the left. They're decked out in school gear, wearing their team spirit in fake tattoos on their cheeks. They're surrounded by other girls, all pretty like my sister, all dressed in school colors, showing their support.

I might not love Barbie and Annabelle, but they know hockey, and they have a group of friends who share the same love for the sport. And here I am, wearing my usual *LotR* hoodie and a pom-pom beanie, feeling like a complete imposter. It doesn't matter that I'm dating Chase, I'm still the weird girl who writes fanfic.

"I heard Lovett has a girlfriend," another girl says.

"Yeah, he's dating some weirdo on our floor, but she doesn't come to his games. She probably doesn't even watch hockey," Barbie scoffs.

"Shh. I think maybe she's in front of us," Annabelle whispers.

"What? Where?" Barbie asks.

I sink down in my seat.

"She probably calls it sportsball and doesn't even care about his position," Barbie scoffs.

"I heard she's obsessed with hobbits or something," Annabelle adds.

"Do you mean hermits? I'd never even seen her before Chase made her into a somebody."

Barbie's voice rings out above me. "She's a loser who doesn't even come to parties because she's always in her room or something. I don't even know if she has friends."

I could move. But then I'd draw more attention to myself. Which I don't want. I wish Tally would get here so I'm not alone, feeling like I don't belong here. Like I don't fit with his friends or teammates.

If I pretend I don't hear them, what message am I giving if I do? That they can continue to shit all over me? Make fun of me because I don't fit in with them?

"Hey, guys." I turn and wave at them. "I didn't see you at the hockey party last week. Probably because Barbie stole Mac's jersey and posted pictures wearing it and got banned from his place. Feels like an exceptionally weird thing to do if you ask me." Apparently that was why they were late-night sprinting out of his house the other week.

Tally, bless her well-timed heart, comes down the row saying *excuse me* and *sorry* to every person she passes. Her expression is one of concern.

"Tally! Hey!" Annabelle waves manically.

Tally waves and gives them a tight smile.

Barbie pales as I move my jacket for her.

Tally frowns as she takes in my face. She glances at Barbiebelle and the rest of their crew, who all look super uncomfortable, and drops into the seat next to me.

"What just happened?"

"I called out the mean girls." My face feels like it's on fire.

Tally's lip curls. She shoots a glare over her shoulder. "Good for you."

They sink into their chairs.

Tally shakes her head and rolls her eyes.

"You're a powerful ally, aren't you?" I muse.

"In this realm, yes. Anywhere else, not really."

"I don't know about that."

The game starts and we turn our attention to the ice.

Tally really knows the game, and she is loud about her feelings. She explains every play to me with genuine enthusiasm. She stands up often and chirps the refs. Hockey in real life is a hell of a lot different than hockey on TV. It's exciting and fast-paced. Chase manages an assist in the second period, which Tally tells me is a really big deal because he's a freshman and they don't get a ton of ice time. We shout and clap, and he gives me a chin tip and a wink after he and Brody slam into each other as they switch places on the ice.

At the end of the game, Tally grabs my hand and pulls me out of the seat. "Come on."

"Where are we going?"

"To say hi to Chase before he goes into the locker room."

I let her drag me through the crowd of people toward the gate where the team files off the ice. A couple of the other players stop to give girls wearing their jerseys kisses before they continue to the locker room. My stomach flips as Chase steps off the ice and removes his helmet. His hair is wet with sweat, his entire face glistens and beads drip down his temples.

I thought naked Chase was hot, but sweaty with exertion in his hockey gear Chase? My entire body approves. Anxiety hits me as his eyes meet mine. I don't know what I'm supposed to do. He steps to the side to allow Brody to pass. He waves as he passes.

"Hey." Chase's smile makes my knees weak.

"You were awesome out there. That was a great assist," I say.

"Thanks, babe. I think having you here was good luck." He pulls off his glove and tucks it under his arm as his tongue drags across his bottom lip. He strokes my cheek with one damp finger and presses his lips to mine. "Sorry I'm all sweaty."

"It's okay."

"I won't be long in the locker room. Will you wait?" He looks so hopeful.

"Of course."

"'Kay, cool. See you soon." He kisses me again, then clomps down the hall, glancing back at me once before he disappears.

"He's so obsessed with you. I love it." Tally links arms with me and we file out of the arena.

We stop in the bathroom and I apply some fresh gloss.

I recognize a few of the girls who were sitting in the same row as me and Tally. I brace myself for their wrath. One girl with red hair steps out. She has a heart-shaped face and freckles across the bridge of her nose. I've seen her behind the counter a few times at the school coffee shop.

She smiles shyly. "I like your sweatshirt."

"Thanks." It's a personal favorite of mine.

"I'm Enid, by the way," she says.

"I'm Cammie and this is Tally."

"You work at the coffee shop on campus, right?" Tally asks.

"Yeah. I do."

"It's nice to meet you," I say.

"You too. Both of you." Her smile is soft and genuine. She worries her bottom lip, like she's shoring up her courage. "It was kind of cool the way you stood up to the mean girls. They're always talking smack about other people."

"They definitely have a lot of opinions," I agree.

"Maybe you'd like to sit together at the next game?"

I finish touching up my lip gloss. "Yeah. I'd like that."

"For sure," Tally agrees. I shove down the anxiety as we leave the safety of the bathroom to wait for Chase in the lobby. Enid says goodbye and joins another girl waiting for her by the door. I have no idea what the fallout will be for calling out Barbiebelle, but I can't worry about it now.

Chase appears a few minutes later, fresh from the shower, wearing dress pants, a white button-down, and a tie. His hair is still wet and he looks totally fuckable. "Hey!" He wraps his arms around me, lifts me off my feet, and kisses my neck.

"Hi." I run my hand down his chest. "You look good."

"We always dress up for games."

Brody and Gage appear behind him, followed by Mac.

"This is my friend Tally. Tally, this is Chase, and his friends Brody, Mac, and Gage."

Brody's head tips. "You know my brother, right?"

"Yeah, and Rix."

"I'm Gage. You're beautiful." Gage holds out his hand.

Tally gives him a tight smile. "I have a boyfriend."

I swear she's only dating that guy so she can use this line without lying.

"I could be your boyfriend."

"You're too young for me." Her blue eyes find mine. "I should go. I have dance practice in the morning. I'll see you in English, though."

"Do you need us to walk you back?" I ask.

"My boyfriend's meeting me outside in like two." Tally hugs me and says bye to the guys.

"How serious is she about the boyfriend?" Gage asks.

"Very," I reply, even though I don't believe that to be true.

"You'll let me know if they break up," Gage says.

"Sure." There is no way in hell I would set Tally up with Gage. I just count my blessings that he doesn't know who her dad is. Yet.

"Who's up for food? I'm starving," Gage asks.

Chase gives me a heated once-over. "You want to just head back to res? I can order something for delivery."

"Don't you want to celebrate the assist?" I ask.

He blinks at me. "Yeah. I do."

I fight a smile.

Brody covers a snort-laugh. "I can bring you something back.

I'll send you a message when we get there, and if you're timely in your response, I'll put in a takeout order for you." He claps Chase on the shoulder. "Nice work out there tonight. Have fun. Play safe."

"Thanks, man."

We head for the south entrance, which means we have to pass Barbie and Annabelle and some of their crew. They glare daggers at me. I ignore them.

Chase frowns in their direction. They all turn their backs. "Do you know what that's about?"

"They were being rude during the game."

"Rude how?" The doors slide open and we step out into the cold night.

I shrug. I don't want to make this more of a thing. Or for Chase to turn around and confront them in a public place like the arena. He can't fight my battles for me.

We make it twenty feet before he grabs my hand and comes to a stop. We're in the middle of a wind tunnel. My hair whips around my face.

"Rude how, Cammie?" Chase asks, more insistent this time.

"They were being mean girls."

His jaw tics. "What did they say?"

I sigh. "They called me a loser and said some generally not-nice things." They seriously know how to hit where it hurts. It's like they have a sixth sense for weaknesses and they dig right in.

"I've had enough of their crap." He takes two long strides back toward the arena.

I rush around in front of him and put my hands on his chest. "Do not make me lay you out. Especially not on cement."

His right eye twitches and his nostrils flare.

I arch a brow.

"Fuck, you're hot." He runs a rough hand through his hair. "It's not cool that they were chirping you."

"I know. And I dealt with it. You can't fight my battles for me, Chase."

"People can be such assholes, though."

"Agreed. But you going in there and sticking up for me won't change anything." I pat his chest. "My insecurities are mine, Chase. Only I can deal with them."

He captures my hand and kisses the palm. "I'm really fucking proud of you."

"I am pretty proud of me, too."

He pulls me into him and folds me in his arms. "Let's go home and celebrate."

"With sex, right? That's what you mean?"

"Yes, Cammie. That's exactly what I mean."

CHAPTER 23

CHASE

"I need to talk to you guys about something important." I nab an extra chair and plunk myself down across from Gage, Brody, and Mac.

Gage mumbles something around a massive bite of burger.

"You look stressed," Mac observes.

"Everything okay?" Brody's already on alert.

"Yeah. No. I don't know." I tell them what happened with Barbiebelle.

"Why are you surprised by this? Those girls are assholes to everyone." Gage shovels a forkful of mashed potatoes covered in gravy into his mouth.

"You're probably going to regret this meal when we're on the ice in an hour," I say, then look to Brody and Mac for…I don't know what. Advice on how to handle this.

"Good for her for standing up to them." Mac is never a fan of the mean-girl nonsense.

"She dealt with them, then?" Brody confirms.

"Yeah, but like…they called her a loser and she was just… apathetic about it?" I run a hand through my hair. "Like she expected as much. Do you think that's why she hasn't wanted to come to one of my games until now?" She always has an assignment to work on. Which is legit, I never *don't* have homework of some kind.

Mac crosses his arms and leans back in his chair until he's balanced on two legs.

Brody and Gage exchange a look. "What was that? What was that look?" I motion between them.

Gage wipes his mouth with a napkin and sets it on the table. "What was your high school experience like, Chase?"

"I don't know, typical? Why does that matter?"

"What does 'typical' mean to you?" Gage presses.

"I played hockey, did well in some classes, did not so well in a few where the teachers didn't think hockey should be my number one. I went to parties, had friends in most groups."

"So high school was a fun ride for you, yeah?" Gage sips his chocolate milk. The guy fucking loves chocolate milk.

"Sure. Yes. That's what high school is supposed to be. Where are you going with this?"

"Do you think Brody's and my high school experiences were the same or similar?"

"I know Brody's was. We hung out all the time." We lived in different parts of the city and went to different high schools, but we played on the same hockey team outside of school and went to a lot of the same parties.

"And me." Gage points to his massive chest. "Do you think high school was fun for a good-looking fucker like myself?"

I roll my eyes. "I'm sure it was."

Gage points to Mac. "And what about this guy?"

"I studied a lot," Mac supplies. "But high school was still fun for me."

"And in the same vein, do you think Barbiebelle had a pleasant high school experience?" Gage stabs a grape on my fruit plate.

"Probably at the expense of a lot of other people's happiness," I grumble.

"Probably." He stares at me.

I stare at him. The dots connect. "You think Cammie's used to this because she was bullied in high school?"

"Makes sense, don't you think?" Gage slurps his chocolate milk and looks to Brody and Mac to back him up.

"She's beautiful in an unconventional way and she's different. She doesn't play by the rules, and she acts like she doesn't give a shit. And girls like Barbie and Annabelle are so caught up in being cool, and having the right friends, and being at the top, that anyone who doesn't fall into line with them is automatically the enemy," Brody says. "You remember Tina, don't you?"

"That girl tried to hump your leg every chance she got." She was at every party. Thankfully she went to school somewhere on the East Coast.

"Don't remind me." He rolls his head on his shoulder, neck cracking. "Think about all the shit she used to pull in the name of getting attention. There will always be girls like that, and they'll bounce around from group to group, spreading their toxicity." He sighs and hangs his head. "And for a while they were a nice buffer from the bullshit, but I feel like it's my fault they're still around all the time."

"I never told them to fuck off, either," Gage says.

"I mostly ignored them." I rub my bottom lip. "I can't have girls like that fucking with my girlfriend all the time."

"She dealt with them, though," Gage reminds me.

"Yeah, but there are always more girls like that out there. What if she can't handle it?" *And what is this horrible tight feeling in my chest?*

Brody raises a hand. "Take a breath. We're freshmen."

"Yeah, but what if..." I hold up a hand. "I know it's a long shot, but what if I get called up? If I go pro, this will only get harder, won't it?"

Gage stares at me like I've sprouted horns.

"I know it's a long shot," I say defensively.

"It's not actually. We're a few months in and it's already pretty fucking clear you and Brody will skate circles around the rest of us," Gage replies. "I just didn't realize you were already head over ass in love with her. She must have a magic pussy."

I grab him by the front of his shirt and lean in. "You do not talk about Cammie's precious."

Gage's eyebrows pull down while Brody's shoot up.

"Her *precious*?" Gage snickers.

"Fuck you, shut up. Don't talk about my girlfriend's body or I will knock your fucking teeth out."

Mac pries us apart. "Stop pushing his buttons, dickhead, and calm the fuck down, Chase."

I take a seat, and Gage smooths out his shirt.

"Everything's fine. Go about your business," Brody calls out.

Mac drops back into his chair, looking smug.

Brody's face is beet red. "Look, Chase, we're freshmen. We have a long way to go before we get to the end of this ride. Which means Cammie has a lot of time to get used to being your girlfriend and all the good and the bad that comes with it. Yeah, she'll have to deal with the Barbies and Annabelles of this world. And they will suck, a lot. There will be puck bunnies, there will definitely be temptation, but if she's your person and you're hers, then you will overcome the obstacles. Give her a chance to grow with you."

"Beautifully said." Mac pats him on the back. "Like a true future team captain."

"Thanks, man." Brody's face remains a shocking shade of red.

"I just don't want her to have to deal with all the bullshit." I want her to enjoy coming to my games. It's special to have her there, knowing she cares and wants to see me play.

"So introduce her to the other partners the next time you invite her out. Talk to Flint and Jason. I'm sure their girlfriends will welcome her into their group. And Tally is good people. I don't know her well, but my brother's fiancée has only nice things to say about her, and Rix is literally one of the kindest, biggest-hearted, most patient people on the planet. I can say that with confidence because she's marrying Tristan, and he can be a well-intentioned but prickly fucker."

"Prickly?"

"He has too many feelings and he doesn't know what to do with them. At least that's what Rix says when he gets all moody." Brody waves the comment away. "Anyway, not the point. Cammie will be one of the WAGs by the end of the year. Give her time and stop panicking about what might happen in four years. Get through freshman year. And buy her some flowers and chocolate or something. Just show her that you have her back, and that you're proud of her for standing up to those girls."

"I am proud of her. I told her that."

"Good. Keep telling her. And still get her flowers."

"Real ones, though. From an actual store." Gage points his fork at me.

"Not the ones from the garden behind res," Mac adds.

"I only did that once."

They arch a brow at me in tandem.

"Okay. Twice. Got it. Flowers. Praise." I feel like I've just gotten a crash course in being a boyfriend from three of the unlikeliest people.

CHAPTER 24

CAMMIE

My finger hovers over the New Tab button on my laptop. "Don't do it, Cammie. Do not open your fic. You do not have time to mess around." I roll my eyes at myself. I should not need a pep talk to finish this freaking creative writing submission. I slump forward and rest my forehead on my desk. "What is wrong with me?"

If I finish this, I have to hand it in. Which is the whole freaking point of writing it. I decide to call my sister, because if anyone can give me a Come to Jesus talk, it's her.

Her face appears on my screen almost immediately. She's in the middle of one of her special masks meant to cleanse her pores. Essie takes skincare very seriously.

"Hey, sorry to video call without warning."

"It's no problem." Her smile turns into a frown. "What's wrong?"

"Nothing."

She purses her lips. "Don't lie. It's bad for your health."

I sigh. "I don't know. I think I'm having an existential crisis." I don't even know what that means, but it feels accurate.

"How about you break that down for me."

I word vomit all my woes, including dragging my ass on the story that's due soon and also the nonsense at the hockey game, and how I'm pretty sure I'm falling for Chase.

Essie claps, her grin so wide it cracks the mask and a few chunks fall off around her smile line. "This is so exciting!"

"I'm over here feeling like I don't have control over anything and you're acting like I've just been crowned prom queen."

"You would never have accepted the title of prom queen," Essie points out.

"That's accurate." I wore a completely black, floor-length, lacy, somewhat gothic-inspired dress to prom. It was a real statement piece. I went with my *LotR* friends as a group. None of us brought dates.

"Okay, I'm going to give it to you straight, no sugarcoating, unless you're feeling too much like a marshmallow, then I'll sugarcoat."

"I can handle straight." I don't really have time for sugarcoating.

"You're scared."

I frown.

"If you finish the submission, you'll have to hand it in. It's your ticket to the creative writing class, but if it doesn't pass their test, you don't get into that course and it's a huge dream for you, so you've spent the past few months writing something else because you're getting the feedback you want."

"Please tell me you're not reading my fanfic."

"I can't do that because that would be me lying, and I don't lie to you." Essie smiles softly. More chunks of mask fall off. "It's amazing by the way. Super well written and very, very hot. And I don't want to know what you've been reading-slash-watching-slash-doing to write such spicy flutter-inducing stuff, but it's awesome. And I can totally understand why you keep posting, because people love it, and you get this wonderful instant feedback."

"Most of the time that's true."

"But this other project will be judged by professors, and that's scary."

I blow out a breath and feel like a deflated balloon. "You're right."

"And it's not much different with Chase. He's the popular jock and you're the adorable elf-loving, quiet girl who doesn't try to fit in with the *cool crowd*." She makes air quotes around the words. "Here's the thing, though, Cam, it takes real guts to go against the grain."

"What if I can never fit in with Chase's friends, though?" It would be so much easier if I were more like Essie and less like me.

"What if you can?" she counters.

"What if they don't like me?" Those girls hit where it hurts every time, and as much as I don't want it to, the sting lingers.

"I'm too high energy for some people and for others I'm a mood lifter. You're not going to be for everyone, Cammie. But if Chase likes you just the way you are, then his close friends probably will, too."

Brody's always been nice to me, and he's Chase's best friend. So there's hope yet. "I think I'm falling for him," I admit. "I don't want to get hurt."

Essie's smile turns empathetic. "Of course you don't. No one does. But falling in love is part of life. And it's amazing and scary and all the best things. Maybe Chase is it for you. Maybe you've found your one. But the only way to know for sure is to jump in with both feet."

"It's kind of terrifying."

"Of course it is. But it can be so amazing, too. Sometimes we have to choose to live life scared, or we're not really living it at all."

"You're right."

"I know."

"Thanks, Essie."

"Anytime, little sis. Can I tell you how excited I am to finally come see you this weekend?" She sets the phone in a holder and turns on the sink.

"Mom and Dad have been messaging relentlessly. I seriously hope they don't embarrass me," I grumble. It's parents' weekend and there is no way Essie will miss out on this opportunity.

"They will one hundred percent embarrass you. But everyone's parents will, so you won't be alone. Will I meet Chase?" She wipes the mask off her face with a wet washcloth.

"Maybe. Probably?" I pull my hood up as realization hits me. "Oh my God, I have to meet his parents."

"I can show up early and perform magic." She flutters her fingers in front of her face.

"But you're coming with Mom and Dad, right? We can just pick an outfit now and I'll do my best with your tutorials for this." I point to my face.

"Sounds good. Take me to your closet."

Half an hour later, my meet-Chase's-parents outfit is chosen, and I have four makeup tutorials to watch.

I sit my ass in my chair and finally, *finally* finish the short story for submission for the creative writing course next fall. The next step is to have it edited, but at least it's drafted. You can't fail if you don't try, but you can't succeed either.

Since I'm on a roll, I tackle an English assignment before I finally hop into my newest chapter. I have new messages from my fic bestie.

@THEREALOPHELIA

Tell me university is better than high school.

@LEGAGORNSANDWICH

Hands down a million times better. Everything okay?

@THEREALOPHELIA

Just the struggles of being the new girl in senior year. I want to fit in, but it's hard when all these people have been together for the past four years.

@LEGAGORNSANDWICH

🙁 That really sucks. At least in university we're all in the same position, brand new, meeting new people, finding friends who are exactly like us.

@THEREALOPHELIA

Fingers crossed I get into Tilton next year. 🤞

@LEGAGORNSANDWICH

It would be so cool! We could fic together!

@THEREALOPHELIA

That would be amazing!

@LEGAGORNSANDWICH

The literal best. And you can finally meet all my friends and my boyfriend!

There's a knock on my door.

I hop up from my desk and check the peephole before I throw it open. "Hi, sexy boyfriend."

Chase grins and bends down to kiss me. "Hi, sexy girlfriend. You ready to grab dinner?"

"Oh crap. It's that time already? Just give me a second." I rush back to my computer.

@THEREALOPHELIA

It would be so cool to have more than one friend on campus when I start university.

@LEGAGORNSANDWICH

Totally! My BF just showed up. Heading out for dinner. Chat later?

@THEREALOPHELIA

Sounds good! Have fun! ♥

"Who's The Real Ophelia?" Chase asks as I exit the chat and close my computer.

"She's my online bestie. We're both obsessed with *LotR*," I explain.

Chase frowns. "How did you two meet?"

"Through fanfic. We read the same fics, and she beta reads my chapters most of the time before I post them. She's a senior in high school."

"How do you know that? Have you met in real life?" Chase presses.

"No, but we talk about school all the time and she's currently reading all the same books I did in my senior year of high school." I slide my feet into my Docs and pull the laces tight.

"What if he's a forty-year-old dude? He could be a high school teacher who's catfishing you." Chase's eyes go wide.

"That's all kinds of problematic for so many reasons. And she's not a forty-year-old dude. She talks like a teenager, not like a forty-year-old trying to talk like a teenager." I pat his chest. "You're being paranoid. It's cute, but also unnecessary."

"Just promise if you decide to meet in person that I can come with you."

"So you can be my bodyguard?" I shrug into my bomber jacket.

"Yes. Exactly."

"Sure thing." I push up on my toes and kiss the bottom of his chin. "You're cute when you're being all protective."

"You mean fierce and alpha, right?"

"Uh-huh."

Chase checks his phone. "Brody and a few of the guys have a table already. They can save us a couple of seats if you want to join them? Or would you rather it be just us?"

The only way to fit in with his friends is to give them the

chance to get to know me and for me to get to know them. "We can join them."

His smile widens and his thumbs fly across the keyboard. "Cool."

We leave my room and he laces our fingers together. We pass Barbie and Annabelle who give us tight smiles. They're still banned from the hockey parties at Mac's and they're definitely not happy about that.

I remind myself that they don't matter. It's better to live life scared than not live it at all.

CHAPTER 25

CHASE

"Look at how neat this room is! And it doesn't even smell like running shoes!" Mom says with genuine pride. She elbows Dad in the side. "Don't you agree? Doesn't it smell nice in here?"

"Yup. Smells great," Dad agrees.

They showed up a good half an hour before anyone else. I took them for coffee in the cafeteria before I brought them up to see my room so Brody had time to shower and get his own shit together.

"Are you boys having fun being roommates?" Mom asks Brody.

"It's been great," Brody replies. "Couldn't ask for a better roommate."

Three nights ago, he wasn't singing that tune when he came back from the library earlier than expected and I was pounding Cammie into my mattress instead of hers. She was mortified and highly apologetic. He reminded me that we had a door hanger for such purposes and maybe I should use it next time, or just have sex in my girlfriend's room, since she doesn't have a roommate.

It was a fair point.

I did not throw my girlfriend under the bus by telling him it was her fault for seducing me with peeks at her new, pretty lingerie. That I took off with my teeth. I just owned that shit like a good boyfriend does.

"Knock, knock, family incoming!" a deep voice booms from the hall.

We all turn to find Brody's dad's broad frame occupying the doorway. Behind him are Brody's older brothers. Based on the shrieking in the hall, someone has already recognized Tristan.

"Hey, Maxine and Cornel! I was hoping we'd see you today!" Brody's dad shakes my dad's hand, and my mom hugs him.

Our parents spent a lot of time together in arenas, trading off driving us to practices, and taking us to out-of-town tournaments over the years.

Brody's middle brother, Nate, slides into the room.

"Can't take that guy anywhere." Nate thumbs over his shoulder and rolls his eyes.

"I love this room! And it doesn't even smell like dirty socks!" A very pretty brunette slides between Nate and Brody's dad and holds a Tupperware container out to Brody.

Brody's eyes go wide. "Please tell me these are what I think they are."

Rix grins. "Oh, yes."

He sets it on his bed and folds her into a hug. "You're the best, Rix."

She smiles up at him. "I have a few premade meals for you, too. Tristan has them."

Brody introduces her to everyone since Tristan is still out in the hall getting accosted by fans. I've seen Rix a couple of times in passing on campus, and she drops off food for Brody every couple of weeks.

Tristan finally steps into the room and pulls the door closed behind him. "Thanks for the save, guys." He glances around. "Wow. I forgot how small these rooms are."

"Especially when there are three hockey players taking up ninety percent of the space." Rix pats his chest.

He gives her a look.

She arches a brow.

The temperature in the room increases by three degrees.

"Can you two stop?" Nate grumbles.

"So when do we get to meet your girlfriend, honey?" Mom asks, apparently oblivious to the weird sexual tension happening between Tristan and his fiancée.

"Girlfriend?" Nate's brows rise. "Locking in early, huh?"

Tristan elbows him in the side and slings his arm around Rix. "Nothing wrong with that."

"She's probably in her room with her parents?" It comes out as more of a question.

"Well, let's go say hi!" Mom grabs my arm and throws open the door.

And of course, because I'm the luckiest fucker in the world, Cammie and her mom and dad and sister—based on how similar they look—are walking down the hall toward my room.

Cammie's eyes flare when she sees me. And mine flare just as wide when I see her. Her sister's arm is linked with hers. She's a few inches taller, and where Cammie is edgy and dark, her sister looks like she stepped out of some fancy influencer account.

"That's her." I pray to the God of Smoothness that I don't embarrass myself and that my parents also don't embarrass me. I raise my hand. "Hi."

Her family stops just outside the door to my room, which is full of people.

A flurry of introductions follows.

"You are just adorable!" Mom says to Cammie. "Chase can't stop talking about how wonderful you are."

"Mom, please." So much for not embarrassing me.

"You're a handsome one, aren't you!" Cammie's mom smiles up at me.

Cammie looks horrified.

At least we're both equally embarrassed by our parents.

"Oh my God!" Rix shrieks as she manages to worm her way into the hall and throws her arm around Cammie's older sister, Essie. "Brody, I didn't realize your roommate is dating my best friend's sister!"

Brody shrugs. "It's a small world, I guess, eh?"

"So small. I love that all my favorite people are connected to each other." She squeezes Essie's arm.

"Hey, Nate." Essie pulls gloss out of her pocket with her free hand and applies it to her lips.

"Hey, Ess." Nate's ears turn red and he ducks his head and rubs the back of his neck.

More introductions happen.

"Should we head down to the lobby?" I eventually suggest because we're totally clogging up the hall and there is literally nowhere to turn in our room without bumping into someone unless we stand on the beds.

"I don't know what everyone's lunch plans are, but I booked us the private room at The Breakfast Bar downtown. They have a killer buffet. You're all welcome to join us if you want," Tristan offers.

"Oh, that is so kind of you! We don't want to intrude, though," my mom says.

"You're not. The more the merrier," Rix assures her. "Plus, I want to catch up with Cammie. I can't believe we haven't run into each other on campus yet."

I look to Brody. He nods.

I turn to Cammie. She shrugs.

"Okay. Sounds good. Let's roll out."

Everyone files out of our room. I pull the door closed behind me.

We divide into two groups and we still fill both elevators.

In the lobby, we pick up Gage and his family.

Barbie and Annabelle almost lose their minds when they realize Tristan Stiles is with us. He signs a few hats and shirts while Rix acts like his tiny bodyguard. Brody and Nate look bored.

Essie keeps stealing peeks in Nate's direction.

Cammie slides her arm through mine. When I look down at her, she crooks her finger and I bend until my ear is at her lips. "Have you noticed how *huge* Tristan's hands are?"

I glance in his direction. Until now, I hadn't noticed. But now that she's pointed them out… "They're like baseball mitts."

"Right? Like dinner plates even." Her nose wrinkles. "Also, my sister is being weird, but we can talk about that later." She squeezes my arm. "Your parents are cute."

I smile down at her. "Your parents are also cute."

"My mom approves," Cammie assures me.

Rix and Essie step in and move our group along so we're not stuck here until tomorrow afternoon.

I kiss Cammie on the cheek and join my parents in their car.

Fingers crossed lunch with the parents isn't an embarrassment fest.

CHAPTER 26

CAMMIE

I figured my parents would meet Chase and his parents for like, five minutes, and then we would go out for lunch and they would ask me questions about them, and then Essie would make me go shopping and try to persuade me to add pastels to my wardrobe.

I did not expect to end up in a private room at some fancy restaurant—which I am sorely underdressed for—with our parents congregated at one end of the table and all the university students and siblings at the other. I ordered a ginger ale because I don't think caffeine is a good idea when I've already sweat through my underpants thanks to the anxiety of all these freaking people.

"I'm going to grab another plate," Tristan says for the third time. "You want anything else, Bea?"

"I'm good for now, thanks, babe." She smiles up at him.

He does this thing with his enormous mitt of a hand that sort of makes it look like he's holding her throat, but then he brushes his nose over hers. She sighs. I look away, because I feel like I'm an interloper on a private moment even though we're in a restaurant.

Essie pulls her lip gloss out for the seven hundredth time in two hours.

During brunch there has been a lot of talk about Tristan and Rix's upcoming wedding, hockey (this is not a surprise), and how we're enjoying university. I mostly listen, fascinated by how obviously obsessed Tristan is with Rix. He's always touching her. And the diamond on her finger is enormous. Just like Tristan's hands. I'm also fascinated by Brody's middle brother. He's quiet, and broody, and ridiculously attractive. But the number of times I've seen him blush in the past two hours is a record breaker. I can't wait to talk about this with Chase. When our parents go back to their hotel rooms tonight.

Tristan drops back in his chair with a heaping plate of food. "Look, Bea, they have cucumber salad." He's the only person who seems to call her this. Maybe it's his little term of endearment.

Rix props her chin on her fingers and smiles at him. "You'll have to tell me if the dressing is as good as mine."

Essie's fork clatters to her plate. Her eyes go wide and she slaps her chest. Her mouth opens and closes like a fish out of water.

"Ess? Are you okay?" I push my chair back.

She grabs at her throat.

"Oh my God!" Rix shoves her chair back. "She's choking!"

Tristan and Nate both push their chairs back at the same time and rise. But Nate bolts around the table and shoves his older brother out of the way. "I got you." He picks my sister up like she weighs nothing, turns her away from the table, and performs the Heimlich maneuver while Essie claws at her throat.

Everyone is freaking out.

A maraschino cherry shoots across the room and rolls behind a plant.

Essie sucks in gasping breaths. Nate sets her down and turns her around, his hands on her shoulders. And then he's cupping her face. I swear they have a moment. And then Essie bursts out laughing. It quickly dissolves into tears.

Rix starts crying too, and then the two of them are howling with laughter.

"What the hell is going on?" Chase asks.

"They're always like this," I explain. I love their friendship. Envy it even.

No one else chokes during lunch. Tristan insists on paying for the whole bill.

As predicted, Essie declares it a girls' afternoon and we split up, all the moms and girls head to the mall for manicures and shopping, and the dads and guys go do whatever it is guys do when they're together. Probably something sporty with this crew. If so, I feel bad for my dad because he's like me and considers reading a sport.

The moms are currently being treated to pedicures, so it's just me, Rix, and Essie. My sister has fully recovered from her choking incident.

"So how serious is this thing with Chase? It seems pretty serious," Essie says as we get our nails prepped for our manicures. "And his mom and our mom are getting along like a house on fire."

I glance over at them. They're bonding like besties. It's super cute. I turn back to my sister. "I think it's pretty serious."

"He seems really into you." Rix sips her cucumber water, takes a selfie while smirking, and sends it to someone. Probably Tristan.

"He brings me flowers and stuff." Mostly from the garden behind res, but he brought me real flowers from a store after I went to his game and stood up to the mean girls. It even came with a note card telling me how proud he was of me in his own semi-legible scrawl.

Essie drops her voice. "And he takes care of your needs—first."

"Oh yeah." I nod while my face starts to turn red. "He's very doting."

"He seems like he would be," Rix says approvingly.

I wish I could get used to how open these two are about sex. I used to eavesdrop when they were in their late teens. The things I learned…

"Hockey boys have great stamina," Rix sighs dreamily.

I nod my agreement while turning seventeen shades of red.

"Have those girls backed off?" Essie asks.

"What girls?" Rix's shoulders roll back.

"Desperate attention seekers who were giving Cammie a hard time," she explains.

"It's fine now." That's not entirely true. They glare at me every time they see me when I'm not with Chase. And more than once Barbie has flicked toothpaste water at me in the bathroom.

Could I take her down? Of course. She's no match for me verbally or physically. But the more I ignore her, the more irritated she gets, which is gratifying in its own right.

"The fucking bunnies." Rix rolls her eyes.

"How do you handle it? Especially when Tristan is on the road?" I ask.

They're getting married next summer, so obviously they've figured out how to make it work and she's not a pile of insecurity all day every day. "It's not always easy. But Tristan and I talk every day and video call when he's away. I have to choose to trust him and let it go. We're honest with each other, and if I'm having a hard day, or there's bunny shit online, he's good about reassuring me. If Chase is the right guy for you, he'll be understanding when you have those kinds of days, too."

"Tristan's super in love with you," I say.

"He is. And I'm super in love with him. Every time I feel my fears creep in, I just remember that loving someone well is a choice, and I'm his just like he's mine." She bumps my sister's shoulder. "Now we just need to find the right guy for Essie."

Essie rolls her eyes. "I've found the right guy for me, like twenty times. They all just decide I'm not the right girl for them. I think I'm swearing off men for now."

She always makes jokes about her relationship history. She's married every single guy she's dated. In her head. Half the reason she moved back from Vancouver was because she started dating another toxic guy and decided the best way to end it was to put a few thousand kilometers between them. Also, she missed home and wanted to be closer to family and Rix.

After girl bonding time and shopping, we head back to campus. My mom meets up with my dad at the hotel—ironically the same one that brought me and Chase together—and Rix and Essie come back to res with me so we can get ready for the hockey game tonight.

All of us are going. I'm excited and nervous.

Tally comes over to my dorm, too, and Essie does all of our makeup.

"Can I just say how much I love that you two found each other on a campus of twenty-five thousand students," Essie says as she expertly gives me the cat eyes I always fail at.

"Right? It's so cool! Like what were the chances?" Tally uses my curling wand on her ponytail.

"I love that our worlds are converging like this and that we all get to hang out together," Rix says with a bright smile. Her phone buzzes and she digs it out of her pocket. "Tristan is asking for an ETA. Apparently, they're at the rink already."

"Of course they are." Essie nudges me out of the chair and beckons Tally over. "Girl, your eyes are unreal." She trades out the black liner for dark blue.

"Should I tell him we'll be there in twenty?" Rix asks.

"If we leave in the next ten, we should be there in twenty." Tally tips her head back and looks at the ceiling while Essie rims her eyes.

"Is the boyfriend coming tonight?" Rix asks Tally.

"He's got a thing," she replies. "Besides, my dad is super

intense about boyfriends so it's better that I keep him out of things tonight."

Essie and Rix exchange a look. I say nothing.

Even with my limited knowledge, I know the boyfriend is kind of a dud.

"You know, Brody is a nice guy," Rix says.

Tally shoots her a look. "I'm aware. I see him all the time in the café. Brody is super hung up on a girl he went to high school with."

"Wait. What? How do you know this?" Rix asks.

"Because we met her before at the hockey game. Enid—remember the girl in the bathroom who wants to sit with us?"

"Of course! I haven't seen her around since then." What a wildly small world.

"Anyway, I overheard her talking to one of the other girls who works at the café. Apparently, she went to the same high school as Brody and she had a crush on him and something happened, but I have no idea what. Anyway, Brody always comes in with Gage and Mac. Gage and Mac always get in line, but Brody mobile orders and does the same hood thing you always do." Tally points at me. "I think it's because he's trying to hide the fact that he's staring at Enid with utter longing. So I know Brody is nice, but dude is pining hard. Plus, I'm not into guys my own age."

"You're dating a sophomore," Rix points out.

"Yeah, but he took a gap year, so he's at least a couple of years older."

"Okay, your eyes are ready for the world." Essie surveys her handiwork.

"Should we head to the arena?" Tally asks.

"Selfie first!" Rix hops up and we all crowd around her phone.

She takes a photo, tags us all with *game ready!*, and posts it to her social media.

Normally, I'd be nervous, but with Tally, Essie, and Rix flanking me, I feel pretty damn invincible. And like I belong.

CHAPTER 27

CHASE

My stomach is staging a revolt. I'm halfway dressed for the game and super fucking thankful that I haven't put on my skates yet, because the way I have to sprint to the bathroom to toss my cookies would have been impossible if I were wearing blades.

"You okay, man?" Brody asks when I return a minute later, embarrassed and a little shaky.

I take a swig of vitamin water and pop a mint. "Just something I ate."

But I ate the same things he did this morning, so that's definitely not it. We're playing one of the best teams in the university league tonight. Last year they handed Tilton their asses in the playoffs, so it's a big-ass game tonight.

"Don't sweat it, Lovett. We've all been there." The team captain claps me on the shoulder, then turns to Brody. "You doing okay?"

"Yeah. I'm used to the hype."

"Bet you are. Can't be easy. You got this." He gives Brody props.

Coach comes into the locker room. "I know tonight is a big night for a lot of you. Especially our rookie players. You want to impress your families, and that's understandable. Remember that you're part of this team, and everyone has a role out there on the ice. Play your part, do your best, and you'll make them proud. Let's get out there and play some hockey!"

The team whoops excitedly and then we're heading down the hall to the rink.

The arena is packed. Everyone cheers and screams as we take the ice. It's a serious rush seeing all these people here. The arena is pretty full during regular games, but this is next level.

I scan the seats, searching for Cammie. I spot Tristan first. He's easier to find because he's massive and a head taller than most of the people in the arena. He's behind our bench with the rest of Brody's family. Mine and Cammie's take up the rest of the row. Our parents are sitting together, and Cammie is insulated by her friend Tally, her sister, and Tristan's fiancée. Which is good because Barbiebelle are two rows back; Barbie is glaring daggers and Annabelle looks uncomfortable. Their place on the social hierarchy has come down a few notches now that they're banned from hockey parties.

"Holy fucking shit." One of the second-year players almost trips over his skates. "Is your brother here?" he asks Brody.

Brody shrugs. "It's family weekend."

Another second-year skates up next to us. "Is that the head coach for the Terror?" He does a chin tip in the direction of Tally.

"Yeah." I nod.

"Holy shit."

"Yeah." I guess this explains why I hurled before we came out here.

There's some real pressure. I just hope I get some ice time and I don't make a fool out of myself if I do. Our opposition takes the ice and we warm up. Brody takes his place next to me at the end of the bench. I wave to my family and Cammie, who blushes, but waves back. She's swimming in one of my Tilton Blaze hoodies, but she looks damn well beautiful.

"I'm really fucking nervous," I mutter.

"I know." He claps me on the shoulder. "Me too, but it's a game like any other. Block out the noise and focus on the ice."

I realize he's probably echoing something his brother said to him before the game. But it's solid advice.

I only get two minutes of ice time in the first period. But Flint, one of the seasoned forwards, gets slammed into the boards in the second period and is pulled for a concussion. Our opposition gets a penalty and I end up on the ice. Some of these guys are three years older and nearly twice as broad as I am. They have years of on-ice advantage. But I have the high of my first game in a packed arena with all the people I care about cheering me on as I glide down the ice. Beans passes me the puck and I deke around players, keeping it out of their possession.

Before I hit the crease, I pass it back to Beans. He takes the shot, but it goes wide and hits the goal post, ricocheting toward me. I act on instinct, lining up the shot. The goalie is already in position, skate scraping across the ice until the blade hits the post. I flip the puck up and tap it while it's in the air. Everything happens in slow motion.

The opposition nudges my shooting arm, hoping to send the puck off course, but it's already left my blade. The goalie's arm extends, his intent to catch the puck, but it skims the underside of his glove, sailing through the space between his pads, crossing the line and hitting the net.

The arena erupts in a chorus of excited shouts. My teammates slam into me, cheering right along with the crowd. I scored my first ever goal for my university team. The high is indescribable. I return to the bench and wave to my family who are beaming, and Cammie, whose lip is caught between her teeth. I wink and she smiles. Brody elbows me. "Stop looking at your girlfriend like that when her parents are right beside her."

"Right. Yeah. Thanks." I seriously hope we get to celebrate later tonight.

The Blaze rides the wave of excitement maintaining the lead

in period two. In the third, Brody stops two goals and manages an assist.

It's an incredible win.

We're basically flying in the locker room. One of the seniors invites everyone back to his place for a party. Our families meet us in the lobby and my mom embarrasses me by getting all gushy and emotional.

I almost die a second time when Coach Vander Zee from the Terror compliments both me and Brody on our game play tonight.

Before anyone else can get between me and Cammie, I close the distance and scoop her up, burying my face against her neck. "Thanks for being here. I know it's not easy for you."

She pulls back, her smile soft and warm as she cups my face in her palms. "So totally worth it." She kisses me, then hugs me again, her lips at my ear as she whispers, "Precious and I will show you how proud we are later."

Life can't get any better than this.

CHAPTER 28

CAMMIE

I wake up to noise in the hall. Giggling and laughing.

I lie there, face mashed into my pillow where the scent of Chase's cologne permeates the fabric. He and Brody got up at a ridiculously early hour for some one-on-one ice time. Scoring that goal has motivated the hell out of Chase. So did the accolades from Tally's dad. He talked about it for days. It was adorable.

I huff his cologne. Usually sniffing him makes me all warm and gooey inside, but today something feels…off. More laughter comes from the hall.

There's a note on the nightstand next to my bed. My stomach twists unpleasantly as I flip it open, preparing for…I don't know. The worst maybe? Which would be Chase suddenly breaking up with me by leaving a note on my nightstand.

Cammie,

I miss you already. Back in a couple hours to grab breakfast with you.

Xo,

Chase

He always dots the "i" in my name with a heart. It's so stinking cute. My smile fades as more laughter comes from the hall. *What the hell is going on out there*? I throw off my covers and pad across the room, pressing my eye to the peephole. Several of my floormates congregate outside my door holding pieces of paper. Several of them are snickering. One guy reads over another guy's shoulder and guffaws loudly.

I don't think through my actions as I throw open my door.

The hallway is full of people. All of them are holding papers in their hands. I glance at my door, trying to process what I'm seeing. Pieces of text-filled paper are taped to my door. The entire thing is covered. Horror, real and overwhelming, hits me hard as phrases pop out at me.

It's my fic. My pen name is at the top of some of the pages, along with the name of the story.

"Oh my God! You're a fucking freak!" one girl says, her lip curling in disgust.

A guy gives me a once-over. "Me and my friends will tag-team you, even if you are a freak."

Someone else takes a picture, likely of my horror-struck face. I'm also wearing a TILTON HOCKEY T-shirt that belongs to Chase. And only a T-shirt.

I slam the door and turn the lock. "Oh my God, oh my God, *oh my God*." I slap a palm over my mouth and back away from the door as tears spring to my eyes.

This is literally the worst possible thing that could happen. I don't even know *how* this could have happened. I also don't know how I'll leave my room ever again.

I pace my room and glance at the window. But I'm on the third floor. I'll break something if I try to jump. I message Tally because I literally don't know what else to do.

I explain in a horribly autocorrected text what's happening.

TALLY

OMW. Be there in less than twenty. I've got your back.

I super duper have to pee, but the noise outside my room only grows louder. This is beyond humiliating.

Less than twenty minutes later a shrill, ear-piercing whistle, followed by what sounds like Colby on a megaphone, nearly startles me out of my skin. As it is, I'm very, very close to peeing my pants. I have to go so bad, but leaving my room is not on the menu while all those people are out there.

A soft knock follows. "It's Tally and…Colby is also here. Everyone else has been told to fuck off, but in nicer words."

I open the door a crack. "Hey." I peek into the hall as Colby shouts into the megaphone for people to get in their rooms or leave the hall with real authority. "I really, really have to pee."

"Let me check the bathroom for you first," Tally offers.

When I'm given the all clear, I empty my bladder. By the time I'm done, she's already pulled all the papers off my door.

"Do you have any idea who did this?" Colby asks.

"I have an idea." I sniffle and blow my nose.

He stares at me. I stare at him.

"Maybe give her a little time to recover from this before you launch an interrogation," Tally suggests. "You could make sure the rest of the pages are down while I talk to Cammie." Tally ushers me back into the room and closes the door in Colby's face. "It was Barbiebelle, wasn't it?"

"Probably, but I don't know ho—" I stop. Close my eyes. Shake my head. "Chase was reading in the common room." Last night I posted the chapter while we were waiting for the Terror game to start. I remember coming into the room and Barbie and Annabelle were standing behind him asking what he was doing. He'd mentioned my name and quickly shut the laptop. But obviously not before they'd seen it.

"Okay. So now people know your fic name. No big deal, right?"

"I write Poly MFM romance."

Her lips pull to the side. "I don't know what that means."

"Two guys and a girl."

She blinks at me. I blink at her. She glances at the pages still fisted in her hand. I try to grab them. She puts a hand out and I briefly consider flipping her over my shoulder to get them.

"Hear me out. Maybe I should read some of this so I can understand why you're the same color as a sheet and also sweaty."

I've already decided I have to dye my hair and change my entire appearance before I can leave this room again. I may need to invest in the pastels my sister is so insistent work well with my skin tone. "Sure. Go ahead."

She takes a seat in my desk chair and starts reading the pages she's holding. "Damn, this is hot." Tally flips the page. "Wait. These are out of order. Maybe I should start at the beginning."

I drag myself off my bed and flip open my laptop. I click on chapter one, then squint at the screen. "I have a bunch of new reviews." Like a lot of new reviews.

"Let me read some of this before you look at them."

I flop down on my bed. "What if Chase breaks up with me because people know I write threesome *LotR*-inspired stories?"

"He already knows about your stories, though. Doesn't he even read them?"

"Yeah, but everyone knows now. And two guys offered to tag-team me already."

"What two guys?"

"I don't know. They were in the hall reading whatever was stuck to my door." I drag a hand down my face. "This is probably just the beginning."

"Fuck those guys." Her lips pucker. "Not literally, though."

Tally falls silent. After a few minutes she mutters, "Oh wow. Holy shit."

I don't say anything. I know the story.

She tugs on her collar, crosses and uncrosses her legs, grips the edge of my desk between page scrolls. "Okay, so now I kind of get the allure."

"Of *LotR* fic?" I ask.

"Of MFM. This is superhot. I mean, I don't know if I'd want to share the actual person I'm deeply in love with, but the fantasy is hot."

"I picture Chase and a second Chase now when I write those scenes," I offer.

Her eyes light up. "Like sweet Chase and dirty Chase?"

"Basically, yeah."

"I can see how that would be inspiring." She closes her eyes. "Yeah, if I envision my fantasy boyfriend times two that would totally do it for me."

I have a feeling her fantasy boyfriend probably isn't her real boyfriend. She goes back to reading.

I pull up my fic on my phone and scroll through the new reviews. Usually there are one or two shitty ones, but several new accounts have popped up and they're ripping apart every single chapter. It's brutal.

"My fic is being flooded with horrible reviews. And some of them have outed my real name. And there's a freaking picture of me with bedhead! How will I ever leave my room after this?" Tears well again.

Tally rolls the chair back and crosses over to my bed. She hugs me and I cry. Then she takes my phone and reads all the shitty things people have said. She also reports the review with the picture of me. "Look, I know right now this feels like the worst thing in the world, but there are three new reviews from people who are in love with this story. And honestly, I can understand why, because it's superhot and until half an hour ago, I wasn't into *LotR* fic and now I'm *super* into *LotR* fic. Like I want my friend Hammer to make us shirts and stuff."

I laugh and wipe the tears away with the sleeve of Chase's shirt. That I'm still wearing. "People are going to be dicks."

"Let them be dicks. Fuck all those assholes. You write hot shit. If you hide from it, you give them power, so take it back and just own it, Cammie," Tally says. "Don't let them win."

"I just...don't want to always be labeled as a weirdo. It'll be like high school all over again."

Tally gives me a small, sad smile. "People love you exactly as you are, Cammie. I do, and I'm pretty sure Chase does even if you haven't said the words yet. I know Essie fits into the cool girl box and that parts of you wish you could be that too. But Essie has her own stuff. We all do. And the grass always seems greener on the other side. I know right now everything feels shitty, but the people who really matter love that you're your own person. Barbie and Annabelle look like they have it together, but they're swans. They have a pretty veneer, but under it all they're struggling too, and they take it out on other people. Show them they don't have the power to knock you down."

"That was an excellent go-get-'em-tiger speech," I say.

"Thanks. I know how it feels to be different, maybe not in the same way, but I still get it. Hiding won't make this go away."

"Okay." I slap my thighs. "Let's get me dressed for maximum don't-fuck-with-me vibes."

Half an hour later—I had to put tea bags on my eyes for ten minutes to calm the redness—I'm dressed and ready to leave my room. If Tally wasn't with me, I don't think I'd be able to do this. Also, I'm trying to intercept Chase before he returns to res so I can break the news before someone else can.

We don't even make it to the lobby without getting heckled.

"This sucks balls."

"Arwen sucks a lot of balls," Tally quips.

I laugh, because what else can I do? "Truth."

We're approaching the front doors when Chase and Brody walk through them.

Two guys high-five them.

Brody and Chase look exceptionally confused.

Chase's face lights up when he sees me, but his brow quickly furrows as a group of girls pass me and Tally, whispering and giggling. One girl calls me a weirdo and another one calls me a slut.

"This is going to be so fun. I might as well get a face transplant."

"Fuck everyone."

"I feel like they already believe that's what I do."

Tally rolls her eyes. "By that logic, everyone who writes murder mysteries should be locked up because they're serial killers."

"This!"

"Lovett and Stiles!" Some guy I vaguely recognize appears out of nowhere. Chase and Brody are still half a room away. "Heard about your girlfriend. Guess I know why you two are so tight." He motions between Brody and Chase. "You ever want to add one more to the party, you know where to find me."

"I wish I had the power of invisibility," I mutter.

"The fuck are you talking about?" Chase asks.

"Everyone knows, man. She's a real freak, huh? Letting you both give it to her." He makes a thrusting motion. "Just like your brother, huh, Stiles?"

Between one blink and the next, Brody has him pinned against the wall with his forearm barred across his throat. Chase jumps in and tries to pry his arm free.

I can't hear what Brody says, but the color drains from the guy's face as he also tries to unbar Brody's arm from his throat.

A group congregates and yells *fight, fight, fight*. People are such idiots.

Chase manages to pull Brody off the guy.

I decide my only option is to step in. The last thing I want is to be responsible for Brody getting suspended from the hockey team because of my freaking fic.

I channel my inner Arwen. "Hey, dickbag," I call out and stroll as casually across the foyer as I can.

His head lifts and his eyes flare as he takes me in. "You have something you want to say to me?"

His gaze darts around. "No, I just…"

"You just what? You heard a rumor and decided it was true? Thought maybe you'd jump on the asshole train and ride it all the way to the station with the rest of the dickheads?"

"I'm sorry. Sorry. I didn't—I—sorry." The guy rushes off.

"Are you okay?" I ask Brody.

He rubs the back of his neck. "Yeah. Are you?"

"What the hell is going on, Cammie?" Chase puts his arm around me.

More people walk by, some whispering. A few guys give Brody and Chase a thumbs up and shout, "Way to go."

"Barbie and Annabelle found out what my fic name was and kindly printed out my story and taped it to my door and the walls and told the entire fucking world," I explain. "So now apparently they believe you, me, and Brody are in some kind of polyamorous relationship." Saying it aloud makes me want to throw up. "I'm super sorry you've been dragged into it."

"I'm so fucking sick of their shit," Brody says darkly.

Chase runs his hand through his hair. "How did they find out?"

I shrug. "Does it matter? Everyone knows now. My entire story is being laughed at and boiled down to just sex and it's so much more than that." I'm on the verge of tears again.

Especially when more people pass and whisper and giggle.

I've turned the coolest guy in my year into the topic of horrible gossip.

No. I haven't done this. Barbie and Annabelle have. Because I have what they want, and they'll stop at nothing to try to take it away from me.

I'm not being even a little paranoid about the whispers and

laughs swirling around us. Rage, fiery and hot, sweeps through me. I'm so done being fucked with.

CHAPTER 29

CHASE

I exchange glances with Tally and Brody as we fall into step behind my furious, and frankly really fucking hot, girlfriend. She stabs the elevator button aggressively.

"What are we doing?" I ask.

"Dealing with the problem once and for all." She tears down several pages of her story from the announcement board while we wait for the elevator of eternity. Two of them have her picture in the top corner.

I pull down three more pages that are too high for Cammie to reach. "Why are they such assholes?"

"They're insecure and want what they can't have," Tally says.

We step into the elevator. Brody blocks people from getting in with us. There are more pages of Cammie's story taped to the walls.

"You don't have to come with me." Cammie shoves her hands in her hoodie pocket.

"We're your backup," Tally assures her. When we reach Barbie and Annabelle's room, Brody steps in front and knocks on their door. Which is a good call.

Barbie opens the door a few inches, all simpering smile. "Hey, Brody! How are you?"

"Oh! It's Brody!" Annabelle yanks the door wide, and Barbie nearly falls over.

I've never seen the inside of their room, but the contents are shocking and damning.

The closet doors are wide open. Barbie scrambles to close it, but we've already seen the many, many photos of me and Cammie taped to the inside. Which is really weird to begin with. But what makes it so much worse is that she's taped her smiling face over Cammie's.

As if that isn't bad enough, there's a stack of copies of Cammie's story sitting on top of her printer, while it continues to whir and spit out more pages. A few flutter to the floor.

"This is the last time either of you will fuck with me." Cammie pans her phone over to the printer, creating video evidence of this sabotage effort, as well as the stalkery-vibes photo collage in her closet. "You will leave my boyfriend alone. You will leave his friends alone. You will not talk about me, look at me, or spread any more lies about me. Because if you do, I will post this video, and I don't think you want anyone to know just how obsessed you are with my boyfriend."

"Maybe you should just post it anyway," Brody suggests.

"Seriously considering it," Cammie quips.

For a moment I consider stepping in, but watching my girlfriend school these mean girls is kinda hot.

Barbie looks like she's about to throw up.

Annabelle is standing in front of her closet wearing a look of abject terror.

The printer finally stops. I'm pretty sure I'm getting a contact high from the ink.

Cammie takes a step closer to Barbie, who basically tries to climb inside her closet. "What kind of lies have you been spreading about me?"

Barbie mumbles something.

"Louder please. So I can hear you."

"That you're sleeping with the whole hockey team."

"Cute. What else?"

"That you get your scenes for your story from Brody and Chase." Barbie swallows thickly.

"Be more specific, please."

"You let them…tag-team you."

"First, so what if I was? It wouldn't have been any of your business anyway. But you decided that because you read it in a story? Or did you think that spreading those lies about me would make Chase break up with me so you'd have a chance to shoot your shot? How's that strategy working out for you?"

"I just—I—I—"

"You just what?"

"It's not fair! You weren't even on Chase's radar until the storm!"

"So this is your act of revenge?" Cammie scoffs. "You ruined your own chance with any of those guys by pulling the shit you did with Mac. I didn't do that. You did. You can take it out on me all you want, but it doesn't change the fact that your actions are the reason you're in this position."

I fall even more in love with Cammie than I already am.

She rolls her shoulders back and puts Barbie in her place. "You have two choices. You can either make a statement to everyone on our floor admitting that you spread false information and lies about me, as well as the guys on the team, and that you are truly and deeply sorry for your actions, or I can post this video. Totally up to you how you want this to play out."

"F-fine! I'll make a statement!" Barbie snaps.

"Great. I'll have Colby call a floor meeting." Cammie gathers the fallen papers from the floor.

Brody, Tally, and I step in to take the rest of the papers from her desk. "Seriously, so many trees died for literally no reason," I mutter.

"Honestly, if you two spent nearly as much time on self-reflection as you do tearing other people down, you might actually be decent human beings." Cammie shakes her head.

We traipse out into the hall.

"That was seriously fucking incredible," I say.

"Okay, well, I'll see you all later." Tally kisses Cammie on the cheek. "Text me when you're not busy."

"I want to be you when I grow up." Brody salutes Cammie and disappears into our room, still carrying a stack of printed pages.

"Can I come to your room?" I rub the back of my neck.

"People will talk."

"Yeah."

"It'll be annoying."

"I can handle it."

"Come on." She nods toward her room. "I have this new scene idea and I want to try something."

"Hell yeah, you do." I lift her up by her waist and throw her over my shoulder.

CHAPTER 30

CHASE

The rumors and the nonsense died down after Barbie got up in front of the entire floor and admitted that she'd been spreading lies about Cammie. It had a domino effect, and it quickly came out that Barbie had been bullying a hell of a lot of people, including her roommate. Annabelle had a complete emotional breakdown in front of the whole floor as she spilled the tea on Barbie and her bullying ways.

It's been two weeks since everyone found out about Cammie's fic, and while the initial reception was mixed, she's gained a whole bunch of ravenous new followers who love her story and can't wait for new updates. There's even a group chat on our floor where they try to strategize how everyone is going to take down Saruman and save the Shire.

Every day I fall a little bit more for her. She's fun and quirky and my favorite person to be around. Christmas break is in a few days and while we don't live super far from each other, we both have a lot of family stuff going on, so I want to get in as much time with her as I can before we head home for the holidays.

Also, I want to bring up moving in together next year.

But one thing at a time.

My phone pings with a new message.

CAMMIE

Handed in the submission for the creative writing course

CHASE

How soon will you be back?

CAMMIE

Already in my room!

I give myself a once-over. I look pretty damn good if I do say so myself. I throw open the door. Gage, Brody, and Mac are in the hall.

Brody smirks. "Nice."

"Couple goals, man," Mac says.

Gage's eyebrows climb his forehead. "You two are a match made in weirdo heaven."

I clap him on the shoulder. "Thanks. Don't wait up." I stride down the hall.

"Halloween was two months ago, bro," some guy says.

"Aragorn!" A girl who reads Cammie's fic high-fives me as she passes.

I knock on Cammie's door.

She throws it open. Her eyebrows lift and her gaze travels over me on a slow sweep that heats as it reaches my face. "My Aragorn."

"My Arwen."

Cammie grabs the front of my shirt and drags me into her dorm room. The door falls closed behind me and she pushes me up against it, dragging my mouth to hers.

"Congratulations on finishing your first round of exams. Also, that new chapter was so hot, I figured we should try out some new stuff to keep things fresh," I mumble around her tongue. "And I'm super proud of you for handing in that submission. I know they'll be begging you to join the creative writing program next year."

"Thanks. I was way too up in my head about it. And I'm so down for trying new things. I've been reading up on interesting positions, but we should probably put my mattress on the floor so neither of us risks an injury."

Her tongue pushes past my lips again, her hands are in my hair, and her perfect body is pressed against mine.

I've definitely fallen for this girl. Hard and fast and out of control. When one of her hands slides down my chest, heading for the drawstring at my waist, I cup her face in my palms and pull back. "Wait."

Her hand freezes on my abs.

"I need to tell you something important." I don't want to freak her out, but I can't keep these feelings to myself anymore.

"Is everything okay?"

"Great. Good. Awesome." I stroke the edge of her jaw. "You're so amazing. The best thing that's happened to me this year."

"You're amazing, too. And so is this Aragorn costume. And this year has been full of a lot of new things for me, and a lot of firsts, and so many of those have been with you and I'm so grateful for that." She settles her palms on my chest. "And you're really fucking sexy as Aragorn." She tries to pull my mouth back to hers again.

"Wait. I'm not done."

She pulls back and bites her lip.

"I know we've only been together for a few months, but I have huge feelings for you. I'm in love with you. I love you." I feel like my throat is closing up while I wait. And also like a case of hives might be in my future if her response is not the one I want. Maybe I should have waited until after the holidays to say this.

"You love me?"

I nod.

The sweetest, prettiest smile lights up her gorgeous face. "I love you, too."

"Yeah?"

"Yeah."

I hug her and bury my face against her neck. "We love each other."

She chuckles and kisses my collarbones.

I pull back and cup her face again. I can't stop touching her. I want to stare at her beautiful face all day long. "Going home for the holidays is going to suck."

"Yeah, but we have a few more days, so we can definitely make the most of them." She runs her hands down my chest. "This is quite the costume."

"There's a store downtown that sells a lot of cosplay stuff. They have a whole wall dedicated to all things *Lord of the Rings*." I lick my lips. "I maybe, might have bought you an Arwen costume in preparation for scene reenactments."

"Legolas has been left out a lot lately," she says softly.

"The last chapter was my favorite."

Cammie smiles. "Mine, too."

Aragorn and Arwen spent a night together in a cave with a hot spring on the way home from a mission. It was just the two of them.

She curves her palm around the back of my neck, and I dip down to capture her lips. We both sink into the kiss, lips parting, tongues pressing forward to tangle. I run my hands down her back and cup her ass. In one smooth motion, I lift her and carry her across the room to her bed. We never break the kiss as I adjust my hand and carefully move her laptop to her desk.

And then I lay her down on her bed. She pulls me on top of her and wraps her legs around my waist. My erection presses against her stomach and we both groan.

"I really love kissing you," I murmur against her lips.

"I really love kissing you, too." She runs her hands through my hair.

"And that, I love it when you do that."

"I love your hair," she compliments. "Please don't cut it over the break."

"I won't. I promise. I love everything about you."

She pulls my mouth back to hers. We make out and grind against each other until we're both breathless and I feel like I'm about to burst out of my skin if I can't touch and taste more of her. We must be on the same page, because she tugs my shirt free from my breeches—that's what the guy at the cosplay shop called them—and runs her hands over my abs.

I pull my shirt over my head, tossing it on the floor.

"I'm a little obsessed with how hot you are in this costume," Cammie says as she loses her shirt.

"That's okay. I'm probably equally as obsessed with you in general," I admit.

I dip down to kiss her again, but she puts her hand on my chest.

I swallow down my nerves. I really hope that wasn't too much truth.

"Just give me a moment to appreciate all the hard work you put into making yourself such a fine specimen of perfect boyfriend," Cammie says as she follows the dips and planes, then smooths her hands back over my chest, pulling me to her.

Our chests meet and all that warm skin touches mine, her nipples peaked against me. We go back to making out, hands on the move. I shift to the right, keeping one thigh pressed between Cammie's as I trail my fingers up her side and skim her breast. She arches into my palm and snakes a hand between us, tugging at the drawstring of my pants—breeches. The moment the bow unfurls, she shoves her hand down the front of my boxer briefs and her warm, soft fingers encase my length.

I break the kiss and press my face into the crook of her neck, groaning. "Fuck, Cammie, your hand feels so good."

"Just wait until you're buried balls deep in my precious," she says in a sultry whisper.

"Can we make love tonight? I feel like tonight is a making love kind of night."

"We can have whatever kind of sex you want." She runs her fingers through my hair again.

My thoughts must be written all over my face because she tacks on, "Except anal."

"I feel like that requires a lot of time, patience, and prep work."

"I feel like that is also accurate," she agrees.

"We'll put a pin in that. We have time to try that later. Much later."

"Okay." She pops the button on her jeans.

"Let me do that." I fold back on my knees, my hands suddenly shaky as I tug the zipper down.

Cammie helps me rid her of her jeans and panties. This time they're plain black. I take off the rest of my clothes while she tugs open her nightstand drawer and grabs a condom. I try to calm the fuck down and not overthink things.

She passes the condom to me. "Hold on a second. We're skipping all the good stuff."

I set the condom on the nightstand and kiss her lips, then trail a path down her throat and over her chest, stopping at her nipples to say hi before I keep going. Most of my bottom half is on the floor by the time I stretch out between her thighs. I loop my arms around her legs and settle in, groaning as I lick up the length of her. "I love the way you taste."

Her hands slide into my hair. "I love your magical tongue."

"I love you, my precious," I whisper against her clit before I circle it with my tongue.

"She loves you, too," Cammie moans.

I take my time, lapping at her, alternating between gentle strokes and hard suction. I ease two fingers inside her and find that spot that makes her gasp and shove a pillow over her face so the entire floor doesn't know what's happening in her room.

Her legs start to shake, and she contracts around my fingers, pulsing against my tongue. I kiss my way back up her body. Cammie tears the condom open and rolls it down my length. I fit myself between her thighs, line myself up, and push in, but just the head at first.

We both suck in a breath, and I lift my gaze to hers. Our eyes stay locked as I sink into her. I'm so right about this being different now that those words have been voiced between us. It's not just about sensation, although that's overwhelming on its own. It's a physical connection that I feel inside my chest. The way I can't look away from her beautiful face. How perfectly we fit together. The way her palm settles against the side of my neck and her lips curve up in a soft, knowing smile.

"God, I love you," I murmur.

"I love you, too."

I'm afraid if I move it will be over before it's even begun, but the need to just *thrust* is too overwhelming, so I pull my hips back and tip them forward, filling her again. We make matching needy sounds.

Cammie hooks one leg over my hip. I slide my arm under the other and draw it up, just like Aragorn did in the last chapter of her story.

"Oh fuck, yes please," she groans.

She tips up to meet my next thrust and grips my shoulder with one hand and my hair with the other. We find a rhythm, moving with and against each other. I can't get enough of her soft moans and quiet pleas for more. Of the way she shudders under me. Or the way her eyes flare and her nails dig into my back when she whispers, "Oh God, Chase. I—I think—I think I'm going to come."

I roll my hips, grinding against her. Cammie's head snaps back and her body quakes as she contracts around me. There's such primal satisfaction in knowing that I'm the one who takes care of her needs like this. That she feels safe enough with me to let go. That I'm special enough for her to let me see her at her most vulnerable and beautiful.

And when her gaze returns to mine, hazy with desire, I let go, too. Falling into bliss along with her.

I collapse on top of her for a few seconds, then realize I'm probably crushing her and push up on one arm. "I think I'm addicted to your precious."

"My precious is also addicted to your mighty sword."

"He is pretty fucking mighty, isn't he?"

"So mighty. The pride of Gondor some would say." She smiles. "I'm so glad our hearts caught up to the rest of us."

I ease out and roll to my side. Removing the spent condom, I tie a knot before I toss it across the room, into the garbage can. "Cuddle time?" I ask hopefully.

"You are such a sap," Cammie observes.

"You love it." Cammie and I wiggle around, shoving the comforter down and pulling it over our naked bodies. She tucks herself into my side and I kiss her cheek.

"You love me."

"I do."

"I love you."

"You do." I can tell she's fighting a smile.

"We should get matching sweatshirts or something," I muse.

"Or you can just write it on the message board on my door."

"When can we move in together?"

Her nose wrinkles. "After first year?"

"We could bring my bed in here and turn it into a double so we'll both fit and get a mattress topper or something." I push up on one arm, excited about the prospect of sleeping beside her every night. "And in the summer we can get an apartment together."

"I don't know that they'll allow us to be roommates, but it's a fun idea. A summer apartment sounds reasonable, though."

I drop back to the pillow. "Right. You're probably right. But won't it be cool to decorate our place *Lord of the Rings* style? And then we can have a queen- or a king-sized bed and no one has to worry about falling off or hitting our elbows on the wall."

"I love this plan."

"Me, too." I'll be her forever Aragorn and she'll be my forever Arwen.

And we'll write our own story, one kiss, one smile, one chapter at a time.

EPILOGUE

CAMMIE

FIVE MONTHS LATER

"If there's a forty-year-old man in that coffee shop, I'm going to knock him out," Chase states emphatically.

"It's a coffee shop in downtown Toronto, Chase. In the business district. There's a really strong chance there's a forty-year-old man in there. Also, you potentially breaking your hand on a dad's face won't be good for your summer hockey program or your criminal record, so maybe just relax."

"I really hope Ophelia is actually a teenage girl," Chase mutters.

"Me, too." I squeeze his hand.

I really hope Ophelia is who she says she is. I open the door to the coffee shop and step inside. Chase presses his whole body against mine. It's cute and also, he's hot when he's being protective.

I scan the tables, looking for a girl my age-ish. Ophelia has been accepted to Tilton and will be living on campus in the fall. I'm starting the fall semester with the creative writing course to which I was granted a placement with huge excitement from the evaluating professor, I'll be living with my boyfriend, and I'll have even more friends on campus. Ophelia and I wanted to meet so we could get to know each other before the beginning of the school year. Chase is chaperoning because he's paranoid that she's an old creepy guy.

My gaze catches on a familiar face. "Tally?"

"Cammie!" She hops up from the table and rushes over to hug me.

There's another girl with her. She has long dark blond hair, deep burgundy lipstick, and a *LotR* shirt with Arwen, Aragorn, and Legolas.

She stands and runs her hands down her thighs, then clasps them in front of her. Unclasps them. Touches her hair. Smiles and her lips pull to the side.

Chase and Tally say hi.

"I'm so happy to see you. Do you live close by or something?" I ask.

Tally went home for the summer. It was the deal she had to make with her parents in order to live in an off-campus apartment next year. It's in the same complex as me and Chase. I'm super excited about it.

"My family lives a few blocks from here. A friend of mine said she was meeting her online friend, and I thought it was a good idea to come with her in case that person ended up being a forty-year-old man."

She and Chase say the last part at the same time.

They smile at each other.

I love them both so much. They're both such caretakers.

She links her arm with mine and Chase hooks his pinkie with my free one.

"Cammie, this is my friend Fee, also referred to as The Real Ophelia. Fee, this is my friend Cammie and her boyfriend Chase."

She raises her hand. "Hey. Hi. It's nice to finally meet you."

"It's nice to meet you, too." I also wave and then we both step forward, then back. "Should we hug?"

"I feel like we should maybe hug?" Fee nods.

And we do. And it feels normal and like I'm hugging my best friend, because that's who she is and has been for the past year. I want to dance and laugh and sway from side to side. My best friend is absolutely not a creepy old man.

Chase grabs us coffees and we all sit at the table.

"This is so wild. I can't believe you two know each other. How do you know each other?" I ask.

All these amazing people who keep stepping into my life are already connected to people I care about. It's like the universe is tying us together in the most amazing way.

"My older sister and Tally's dad work together."

"Your sister works for the Terror?" Seriously. For a person who had only watched hockey with my sister and Rix, I seem to draw a lot of hockey people into my orbit.

"She's the new assistant coach."

"Oh wow. That's wild."

"What's wild?" Chase slides into the seat next to mine and sets a coffee in front of me. Then kisses me on the cheek.

"That my favorite people are right here with me, and we're all connected by hockey and spicy stories."

If someone would have told me I'd end up dating a hockey god and finding two amazing friends a year ago, I would have laughed in their face. Now I can't imagine my life without any of them.

First year was amazing, but second year is shaping up to be one for the books.

Join my newsletter for a Chase and Cammie bonus scene!

ABOUT THE AUTHOR HELENA HUNTING

NYT and USA Today bestselling author, Helena Hunting lives on the outskirts of Toronto with her amazing family and her adorable kitty, who think the best place to sleep is her keyboard. Helena writes everything from emotional contemporary romance to romantic comedies that will have you laughing until you cry. If you're looking for a tearjerker, you can find her angsty side under H. Hunting.

OTHER TITLES BY HELENA HUNTING

THE TORONTO TERROR SERIES

If You Hate Me

If You Want Me

If You Need Me

If You Love Me (Coming March 2025)

THE PUCKED SERIES

Pucked (Pucked #1)

Pucked Up (Pucked #2)

Pucked Over (Pucked #3)

Forever Pucked (Pucked #4)

Pucked Under (Pucked #5)

Pucked Off (Pucked #6)

Pucked Love (Pucked #7)

AREA 51: Deleted Scenes & Outtakes

Get Inked

Pucks & Penalties

Where it Begins

ALL IN SERIES

A Lie for a Lie

A Favor for a Favor

A Secret for a Secret

A Kiss for a Kiss

LIES, HEARTS & TRUTHS SERIES

Little Lies

Bitter Sweet Heart

Shattered Truths

SHACKING UP SERIES

Shacking Up

Getting Down (Novella)

Hooking Up

I Flipping Love You

Making Up

Handle with Care

SPARK SISTERS SERIES

When Sparks Fly

Starry-Eyed Love

Make A Wish

LAKESIDE SERIES

Love Next Door

Love on the Lake

THE CLIPPED WINGS SERIES

Cupcakes and Ink

Clipped Wings

Between the Cracks

Inked Armor

Cracks in the Armor

Fractures in Ink

STANDALONE NOVELS

The Librarian Principle

Felony Ever After

Before You Ghost (with Debra Anastasia)

FOREVER ROMANCE STANDALONES

The Good Luck Charm

Meet Cute

Kiss my Cupcake

A Love Catastrophe

www.ingramcontent.com/pod-product-compliance
Lightning Source LLC
Chambersburg PA
CBHW010833080125
20037CB00002B/3